READ.
INTO THE MILLENNIUM

READ

INTO THE

MILLENNIUM

TALES OF THE FUTURE

o   o   o

From the Editors of READ Magazine

The Millbrook Press
Brookfield, Connecticut

Library of Congress Cataloging-in-Publication Data
Read into the millennium : tales of the future / from the editors
of Read magazine.
p. cm.
Summary: A collection of science fiction short stories and
excerpts from longer works by a variety of authors including
H.G. Wells, Isaac Asimov, Fredric Brown, and Lois Lowry.
ISBN 0-7613-0962-4 (lib. bdg.).
1. Science fiction. 2. Children's stories. [1. Science fiction.
2. Short stories.] I. Read magazine.
PZ5.R198417   1999
[Fic]—dc21   98-8390   CIP   AC

Published by The Millbrook Press
2 Old New Milford Road
Brookfield, Connecticut 06804

ACKNOWLEDGMENTS

"April 2000" reprinted by permission of Don Congdon Associates, Inc. © 1948 by Love Romances, Inc., renewed 1975 by Ray Bradbury. Originally printed as "Mars is Heaven!" in *Planet Stories* in Fall 1948 and later collected in *The Martian Chronicles*.

"By the Waters of Babylon" from *The Selected Works of Stephen Vincent Benet* by Stephen Vincent Benet. Holt, Rinehart & Winston, Inc. Copyright © 1937 by Stephen Vincent Benet. Copyright renewed © 1965 by Thomas C. Benet, Stephanie B. Mahin, and Rachel Benet Lewis. Reprinted by permission of Brandt & Brandt Literary Agents, Inc.

"Future Tense" by Robert Lipsyte, copyright © 1984 by Robert Lipsyte. From *Sixteen Short Stories*, edited by Donald

Read is a literature magazine published for students in middle and senior high school by the Weekly Reader Corporation. Published biweekly during the school year, the magazine features the best of contemporary young adult fiction and nonfiction with classical literature adaptations and historical theme issues. The Best of *Read* series celebrates the magazine's fiftieth anniversary.

INTRODUCTION

Imagine a gathering of writers. This panel of creative minds includes Frankenstein's mother, Mary Wollenstonecraft Shelley, as well as the inventor of the Time Machine, H. G. Wells. Seated beside them are Ray Bradbury, Isaac Asimov, Kurt Vonnegut Jr., Lois Lowry, and Robert Lipsyte. They and others have come together at the dawning of a new millennium to debate a most intriguing question that concerns us all: *What is the future and how will it change us?*

"Beware science!" Mary Shelley warns, "for what you create will one day destroy you!"

Lois Lowry, creator of a fictional prophet called the Giver, might disagree. "Beware conformity," she'd say. "It is sameness—not science—that will erase your memories and your humanness."

Kurt Vonnegut Jr. might lean forward earnestly to offer this practical advice, the same he gave to the graduating class of Massachusetts Institute of Technology in 1997: "Wear sunscreen. If I could offer you only one tip for the future, sunscreen would be it. The long-term benefits of sunscreen have been proved by scientists, whereas the rest of my advice has no basis more reliable than my own meandering experience."

In the year 2001, *Read* magazine, published by Weekly Reader Corporation, will celebrate its fiftieth year of publishing. To mark this milestone, the editors of *Read* are proud to bring you this collection of science-fiction stories. These tales of time machines and robots are more than just make-believe fantasies about the future. They are a reflection of the times in which they were created. Ray Bradbury, whose imagination has taken him to Mars and back many times, tells us in his *Martian Chronicles* that when we gaze into the river that is the future, the reflection we see is ourselves—our worries, our failures, but also our desires and our sincerest hopes.

The millennium is both an end and a beginning. Will the twenty-first century bring with it a new world peopled with Elois, as H. G. Wells suggests? Or will the future be a place where all the memories of the past are stored in the mind of the Giver and where the Handicapper General ensures no one is better than another?

The distinguished panel of writers are here, bound between the covers of this book. They are ready and waiting to tell their stories. Simply turn the page . . . and the debate will begin.

CONTENTS

Part 1

WHAT WAS THE FUTURE

*In the eighteenth and nineteenth centuries,
the marvels of science and modern technology
were wonderful . . . and frightening.*

THE TIME MACHINE

THE NEW PROMETHEUS

PART 2

WHAT IS THE FUTURE
Today, the future is alien indeed.

PART 3

WHAT WILL BE THE FUTURE

In the twenty-first century and beyond,
the future will exist in the minds—and
memories—of the dreamers.

PART 1

WHAT WAS THE FUTURE

□ □ □

In the eighteenth and nineteenth centuries, the marvels of science and modern technology were wonderful . . . and frightening.

THE TIME MACHINE

ADAPTED BY SCOTT INGRAM
FROM THE NOVEL BY H. G. WELLS

o   o   o

**The Eloi lived in a lush paradise
where everything they require was simply
provided. But there was another world,
a frightening underground world of
Morlocks and darkness.**

On a chilly winter evening in London, England, in 1895, wealthy friends gather for food and conversation. They sit by the fire and watch as George places a darkly varnished box on a table. "Listen carefully," George begins. "I believe that our ideas about the dimensions of this box are false—or shall I say—incomplete."

"The cube has three dimensions," says Walter Goodwin. "Length, width, and height. What more is there?"

"Time," says George.

Walter laughs. "You're claiming that time is a dimension?"

"Precisely!" George answers. "Length, width, and height are defined as planes being right angles to one another. I say that time is at a right angle to those other three dimensions. See?"

Donald Filby admits he is a bit muddled. George picks up the box.

"The cube exists *now*. If it didn't exist in the *now*, well then it could not have length, width, or height."

Another friend who has listened to this point, now speaks. "If time is a fourth dimension, George, then why is it that we cannot change time as we do length, width, and height?" asks Dr. Millard. "We can make that box smaller or bigger, but we cannot change what you call the *now*."

"Are you so sure, doctor? Perhaps it is possible to move through time the way a fish swims through water," George answers with a smile.

"Impossible!" says Donald Filby.

"What if I could give you proof?"

The gentlemen in George's parlor gaze at him with smiling eyes. "One cannot move from the present moment to some other time," says Walter. "At least not physically."

"That, my good friend, is where you are wrong." George puts another log on the fire. Then he opens the box and removes a small object that resembles a horse-drawn sleigh. It has a glittering metal frame and a cylinder at the front made of ivory and crystal. Two small levers extend from the cylinder toward a seat. The toy—for that is what it looks like—is actually a miniature of a much larger machine, George tells his curious but skeptical guests. "A machine," he says, "in which to travel through time."

The gentlemen gather closer to the "toy" George now sets upon the table. One lever, he explains, when pushed forward sends the machine into the future. The second lever reverses direction.

"Preposterous!" Walter exclaims.

Smiling, George takes Walter's finger and places it on the forward lever of the small machine. "Watch carefully," George says.

George presses Walter's finger. A sudden breath of wind gusts through the room. Candles flicker. The machine slowly disappears.

An uneasy silence settles over the room as the men try to grasp what they have all seen. Dr. Millard appears angry. "Look here, George! You are making fools of us. You don't really think we believe that little toy has disappeared, do you?"

"No, it has not disappeared," George admits.

"It is in the same place—just in a different time."
He smiles at his friends. "As I will be, if all goes as I
have planned."

"Do you mean to suggest that you are going to
attempt to travel through time?" Donald asks.

"The larger model of my little 'toy' is in my
laboratory," George says.

"Preposterous!" Walter repeats and turns away.

A week later, however, the gentlemen gather
once again at George's home. They have been in-
vited for dinner. The dining room table has been
set and a steaming roast of beef is on the sideboard.
Two servants stand, near the doorway, ready to serve
the guests. Dr. Millard turns from the fireplace
where he has been waiting for George to arrive. "It's
half past seven now," he says. "I have a letter here
from George that tells us he may be late and that
we should begin to eat. He says he'll explain when
he arrives."

The men sit at the table. No sooner is the beef
carved and served than George appears in the doorway that leads to his laboratory. His coat is filthy and
torn. His face is pale, with a deep cut on the chin.
He staggers into the room and collapses in a chair.

"Good heavens! George! What happened?"
Donald Filby cries.

"Water!" Dr. Millard orders and a servant returns with a pitcher. George gulps the water from his glass.

"What on earth have you been doing?" asks Walter.

George shakes his head. "I'm starving," he answers.

A servant quickly sets a plate before him. At once, George begins to cut and eat his meat. "I . . . I've had the most amazing encounter," he says while chewing. He drinks a bit more water. "I was in my laboratory this morning, but since then, I've traveled 8,000 years!"

The gentlemen seated around the table exchange worried glances. Their good friend sounds delirious.

"I pushed the lever," George says.

Dr. Millard leans forward. "What lever?"

"To the future, of course. I had to discover what price humans might have paid for the follies of today," George answers. He reaches for a second helping of food. "What if," he begins again, "what if our species had lost all humanity and become uncaring brutes?"

"Are you saying that you have traveled through time?" Walter asks.

George nods. He remembers the nightmarish sensation of falling at the moment he pushed the lever forward. Then the sun leaping across the sky hypnotized him. Night seemed to follow day like the flapping of a huge black wing. Then the changing of so many nights and so many days became a whirling grayness. He slipped through time like a vapor until at last he tugged on the level to stop his journey. The machine indicated that 8,000 years had passed.

The gentlemen sitting around the table are dumbfounded. Could their friend be telling the truth? "Really, George," says Walter at last. "Do you expect us to believe that—"

"Let me finish!" George says. He mops the perspiration from his brow. "To argue with you over the truth will cloud the picture from my memory!"

"Yes," says Dr. Millard. "Let him finish. I want to know what our Time Traveler has seen in the year 9895."

The gentlemen settle back in their chairs and listen.

o   o   o

The Time Traveler is lying near a thick stand of bushes beside his overturned machine. A raging storm crashes around him. George is muddy, soaking wet, but unharmed. He gets to his feet. Nearby is a huge statue, carved from stone. At its base are thick metal doors, tightly closed. The statue resembles another from Earth's past—the Sphinx of ancient Egypt. George stares and wonders if the people of the future worship such idols.

He attempts to right his machine but slips and gashes his chin on the machine's handrail. Through his pain, George slowly becomes aware of voices in the bushes. He reaches for the levers of his machine, ready to return to his own place and time, but then he hesitates. He has come to meet the future of humanity. He cannot turn now and flee like a frightened dog.

The foliage rustles and suddenly, humans separated by hundreds of centuries stand face to face. They are shorter than George, who stands nearly six feet tall. They giggle shyly, like small children. Their skin is ghostly pale, almost bloodless. They are dressed only in tunics and sandals.

George speaks first. "I am . . ." How shall he explain? "I am George."

A young man steps forward and speaks in primitive English. "I am Lorac. Did you fly here on the angry clouds?"

"I do not ride on the clouds," he answers. "I have come here across the years."

"Years?" Lorac asks. "What are years?"

Such a childish question surprises George. He had expected more from future humans. "Why years are a measure of time," George explains.

Lorac says nothing more. He seems uninterested. A young woman approaches George and drops a chain of flowers around his neck. She is beautiful. Her skin, like the skin of the others, appears so smooth and soft that George wonders if these future humans do any work.

"I am Weena," the woman tells him. "The flowers are for you to wear."

"Thank you," George replies. "Who . . . that is, what are your people called?"

"We are the Eloi," Weena answers and smiles. She beckons him to follow.

George removes the important levers from his machine and follows the Eloi through a mass of green shrubs and tangled blooms. London has become a paradise. The flowers are deep green and lush. Some flowers measure a foot across.

Near the bank of a rushing river, the Eloi rest. Some pick wild fruit to eat. George studies the orange-sized berry. "Do you grow these berries?"

George asks one of the Eloi sitting near him. "Who plants and tends to your food?"

The Eloi answer simply, "Food is always here."

George thinks a moment. "Your clothes—who makes them?"

"You ask many questions," the Eloi says.

All at once, George hears screams from the rushing river. He sees Weena being swept downstream. He jumps to his feet, but none of the Eloi hurry to save her. Some giggle. Some turn away. George doesn't hesitate. He dives into the water and struggles through the current. He pulls Weena to shore, and the two collapse into a heap, gasping for breath.

"What kind of world is this," George wonders, panting, "where life has no meaning?"

Weena smiles weakly at George. "Thank you for pulling me from the waters."

"Why did no one try to save you?"

"Save me? Why?" she asks.

"Doesn't anyone care if another person is drowning?" he asks, flabbergasted and a bit angry.

"I do not know what you mean by *care*," she says.

Suddenly, Lorac points at the horizon. "The sun sinks! Hurry!"

Weena scrambles to her feet. "Come," she cries, pulling George's arm. "Hurry. The shadows grow long."

She leads him with the other seemingly panic-stricken Eloi towards a large domed building on a hillside. Inside, are tables filled with fruit. Oranges are the size of watermelons; grapes, as large as fists. George has never seen such bounty. The Eloi are now safe inside the dome. Their panic has subsided. They eat hungrily.

"Weena, why is it so important for you to hurry inside?" George asks.

"The Morlocks come in darkness. They live in the ground."

George finds it hard to believe that future humans lack strength and intelligence and are afraid of the dark. The idea seems absurd. "Why do you not build fires to protect you at night?"

Lorac has been listening. Now he asks, "What is fire?"

George feels his pockets and pulls from one a box of matches. He strikes a match and it flames with a sizzle. "This is fire! Do you not cook your meat with fire?" The Eloi stare, fascinated at first as George strikes one match after another. Soon, though, their fascination wanes. They turn away.

George realizes that they have no understanding of the importance of fire, nor do they have the curiosity to even learn, to question as he has been questioning them.

He has seen enough. He walks towards the door and pushes it open. At once, the Eloi scream and Weena tugs at his arm. "Do not go out. The Morlocks!"

George looks into her eyes and believes he sees a dim look of caring. "Come with me, Weena."

"Take this," she says and slips a handful of small, oddly shaped flowers into his coat pocket.

George walks away into the night. He returns to the spot where the machine should be, but it is gone. He searches the wooded area nearby, then sits. In the darkness, his search is futile. Suddenly, he feels a light touch on his face, as if a spider has brushed across his cheek. He rubs it away. The feathery touch does not stop. Then George feels a tugging at his sleeve. He spins around and sees dozens of luminous red eyes staring at him from the blackness.

"Who's there?"

The sound of snapping twigs is the only reply. He feels something clutch at his ankle.

"Stop!" He kicks. "Get away!"

He fumbles in his pocket for the remaining matches and lights one, then chokes back a scream. He is surrounded by ghostly white, hairy, half-human creatures with glowing red eyes. Larger than the Eloi, they have red, daggerlike teeth. They are the Morlocks. The match light dims, goes out. George strikes another. He hurries to build a fire. As the flames lick and flicker, the Morlocks retreat into the darkness.

◦ ◦ ◦

Hours later, George is asleep when he feels a hand on his face. He lashes out with his fist. A woman's cry brings him to his senses. It is nearly dawn. His fire has died to warm embers. Weena crouches near it, cupping her chin where George has struck her. "Weena, I'm so sorry. I thought you were a Morlock."

"I am glad you are safe," she says. "I was afraid for you."

George smiles. Gladness and fear are human emotions. Perhaps the Eloi are capable of feeling but are ignorant of their emotions just as they are ignorant of fire.

In the early morning light, he sees tracks leading from the spot where his machine upturned in the bushes to the metal door of the giant stone statue. The doors are tightly sealed. George turns to Weena. "Is there another way inside?"

She nods, then says, "But you must not go. You will never come back! When you opened the door, Lorac and Selim went out, too, into the night. They are gone now. You will disappear like them and never return."

George takes her hands. "Listen to me, Weena. I can save your friends, just as I pulled you from the waters yesterday. Show the way."

Reluctantly, she agrees. She takes him to a large open field in which are large wells. Weena hangs back, trembling. George peers into the dark hole. Warm, foul-smelling air blows into his face. George understands that the wells are air shafts. He hears distant rumbling. The Morlocks must live in some subterranean chamber or caves. He lowers himself into the opening.

His fingers dig into the nubs of stone as he descends, a spider on a wall. Above him in the sunlight is the world of the "haves," the Eloi's world of plenty, a paradise. Below him in the horrid dark is the world of the "have nots," the Morlock's world. Yet, the Morlocks seem to possess some curiosity and intelligence. They built this chamber, these ventilation shafts, and the rumbling generator that sucks fresh air below. And they have stolen his machine.

His eyes have adjusted to the darkness. He sees now that the shaft descends even farther down, but a tunnel cuts across it. He reaches his foot to the floor of the tunnel and cautiously makes his way. He follows the wormlike tunnel until it widens. At last he comes to a ledge that overlooks a vast underground chamber. He can distinguish through the shadows several Morlocks seated at a crude stone slab, used as a table. They appear to be eating meat! What animal, George wonders, survives in the dark to serve as meat to the Morlocks. Then he knows. Against the wall, chained by the ankles, is Lorac. The Eloi! They are the Morlocks' human cattle, fed and fattened and taken in the night.

Disgust and anger fill George but before he can think to act, something grabs him from behind. George struggles, breaks free, then reaches for the only weapon at hand—a large rock. He smashes the melon-soft skull of his Morlock attacker. The sounds of the struggle have alerted others. As they climb the walls to reach him, George realizes that his only hope of escape is fire. The matches are in his pocket and yet he has nothing to burn. He grabs the wooden club from the dead Morlock's hands, then makes a torch from the Morlock's thin tunic and greasy hair. The sudden fire startles his pursuers and keeps them at bay.

George waves the torch. "Get back! Get back, you devils!" He descends a narrow staircase to where Selim lies, dazed from a head wound. A Morlock tackles him from behind. George pitches forward and drops his torch into a pool of oil used to fuel the ventilation pump. The oil bursts into an inferno. The terrified Morlocks howl and run toward the metal doors. The fire blinds them; the smoke suffocates them. Those that survive, fall forward through the doors, shielding their weak eyes from the blinding sunlight.

Below, in the black smoke, George uses a rock to smash the chains that pin Lorac to the wall. "Sleep," Lorac mumbles.

"Get up, you fool. We'll be roasted alive!"

George drags him away from the metal doors and into another chamber. The thick smoke singes George's eyes, but he can still make out the daylight at the far end of still another tunnel. He and Lorac crawl. The agonizing cries of the dying Morlocks echo in the chamber behind them.

The tunnel widens into a small chamber, a cave. And there George finds his time machine. He turns to Lorac. The Morlocks have not followed them.

"Go! Return to the Eloi! Tell them the Morlock's world is destroyed." Lorac nods feebly. George presses the matchbox into the Eloi's small hand. "Fire," he tells him. "Remember. Fire."

As smoke billows in black clouds through the tunnel, Lorac escapes through the mouth of the cave. George quickly assembles the two levers onto his machine, then pulls the lever to reverse time.

o   o   o

At the dining room table, George slumps in his chair. Telling his tale has exhausted him even more. The other gentlemen are silent. A clock in the corner ticks loudly. Finally, Dr. Millard clears his throat. "Eloi and Morlocks . . . all of this exists right here in London, in this place."

"But not in this time, yes," George says.

Donald Filby removes his pocket watch and exclaims, "My goodness. It is one o'clock in the morning! Where has the time gone?" He chuckles uncomfortably, realizing his words hold a different meaning for poor George.

"Yes," Walter says, standing. "We must go. Let's give George some rest. It's not everyone who has an 8,000-year day."

George lifts his head. "Laugh then. Go ahead. But how do you explain these?" He removes from his pocket the wilting flowers given to him by Weena. "You're a botanist, Dr. Millard. Tell me, what species of flowers are these?"

Dr. Millard picks one up. After a few moments, he admits he does not recognize the flowers. "Of course, I would have to study them further before making any conclusion."

George pushes himself to his feet. "Come, look at my machine."

Walter sighs. Donald Filby shrugs. Dr. Millard nods. The gentlemen follow George into his laboratory. The machine is outside the double doors.

"I don't see any tracks on the ground," Walter says.

"It is exactly where it was when I left the inferno in the Morlocks' chamber," George says. "It traveled through time, not space."

The gentlemen leave quietly.

The next morning, Donald Filby returns to George's house. He has spent a sleepless night worrying about his friend. A servant opens the door and allows Donald to go into the laboratory. Things are amiss. Books have been tossed from the shelves. Papers flutter in a cold breeze from the doors left open to the courtyard. Donald hurries outside. The time machine is gone. The ground shows no tracks to indicate that the machine has been dragged or driven away.

Confused, Donald turns and enters again the laboratory, closing the doors now behind him. Then he spies on the laboratory table the cluster of strange white flowers George had shown to Dr. Millard.

Donald picks up one of the blossoms. "I understand," he says aloud. "Even though their minds and strength are gone, gratitude and tenderness still live in the hearts of the Eloi."

THE NEW PROMETHEUS

BASED ON THE NOVEL *FRANKENSTEIN*
BY MARY SHELLEY

◦ ◦ ◦

In Greek mythology, Prometheus gave the gift of fire to humankind. Now Victor Frankenstein was about to give the world a new gift—immortality.

On a dreary November night, 1815, in a laboratory in Switzerland, Victor Frankenstein is about to complete an experiment on which he has toiled for two years. The brilliant university student is alone in his laboratory. He stands over a grotesque body lying on an operating table. The Greek mortal Prometheus brought the gift of life—fire—to man. Now Dr. Frankenstein is about to give the world an even greater gift—immortality.

In glimmering candlelight, Victor gathers his instruments around him. He works feverishly. So many wise scholars before him had searched for the secret of life and failed. Now Victor Frankenstein has found the answer. He sends a spark of life into the motionless body, a dead carcass made from graveyard parts. He waits . . . one minute, two minutes . . .

One dull eye opens. The creature breathes hard. Its muscled legs jerk convulsively and then are still.

"It moves!" Victor gasps.

The creature opens both eyes and stares vacantly upward, not yet seeing the scientist above him, not yet comprehending its surroundings—the vials of fluid, the operating table, the dim walls of the laboratory. The creature's mouth gapes open, gasping for breath. At that moment, repulsion fills Victor. He sees now that the creature he has created is a monster. Its lips are shriveled and black. Its yellowish skin scarcely covers the huge framework of sutured muscles and arteries.

"What have I done?" Victor cries. "No, no! I cannot do this."

He sweeps his instruments from the table. As the creature strains against the ropes that bind him to the operating table, Victor sets fire to his laboratory notes. Then he flees, leaving the pathetic creature to be devoured by the spreading flames.

0   0   0

A church bell strikes six. Rain falls heavily on the city just now awakening. Victor has wandered aimlessly all night through the streets, stopping now and again to look fearfully over his shoulder. A coach drawn by two horses thunders toward Victor. He falls backward, inches from the horses' hooves and the carriage wheels.

The carriage stops and a man leaps out. "Are you hurt? Here, let me help you," the man kneels beside Victor, moaning on the cobblestones. Suddenly, the man freezes in shock. "Victor? Is that really you? It's me, Henry! Henry Clerval."

Terrified, Victor seizes Henry's arms. "Save me!"

"Save you? From what? Victor, you're shaking."

"I've done something dreadful. Something . . . evil!"

"You aren't making any sense. You're ill! Here," Henry helps Victor to his feet and leads him to the carriage, "you must get out of this rain."

Still, Victor clings to his friend. "We must leave the city at once. Please, take me back to Geneva. Quickly!"

Henry shakes his head. "You are in no condition to travel to Geneva. You need a doctor."

Victor attempts to argue but is too weak. He collapses in Henry's arms.

That night, while Victor sleeps in his bed, the doctor summoned to the student's apartment informs Henry that his friend is suffering from brain fever. He is exhausted, both mentally and physically, the doctor explains.

"We suspected something might have gone wrong," Henry says. "His father sent me to find him. He had not heard from Victor in almost two years. Doctor, I must admit, I was shocked to see him so pale, so thin." Then Henry adds, "And so terrified. What could have frightened him?"

The doctor sighs. "I do not know. But many times I've seen your young friend in local butcher shops and in the hospital dissecting room."

"The dissecting room?"

"Yes, where body parts are discarded after an operation."

"But why would Victor be there?"

The doctor shrugs. "I suppose it is one way to learn about human anatomy. We are on the threshold of an exciting time in science, Mr. Clerval. We are learning so much so quickly." Again the doctor sighs. "Perhaps too quickly."

"Science has always been Victor's passion. When we were younger, he often told me that he believed he was destined to accomplish some great thing. Victor wanted so much to help humanity. He believed science was the method of achieving that."

"Yes, I've heard that he was a very promising scientist, quite brilliant some have said and yet his ideas . . ." The doctor frowns. "It's quite unfortunate that he was expelled."

This news startles Henry. Neither he nor Victor's father had any idea that Victor was no longer attending classes. "Are you saying the university forced him to leave?"

"It concerned some nasty business about transplanting the brain of one animal into the body of another," the doctor explains.

"Transplanting? Why, I've never heard of such a thing. Surely, it can't be done!" Henry says.

"Whether it can be done is not the question," the doctor answers. "We must ask ourselves whether it *should* be done. Science may propel us swiftly into the future but with what consequences? A brilliant student exhausted to the point of delirium." The doctor shakes his head and prepares to leave. At the door, he turns with a final remark. "I'm glad to learn that Victor Frankenstein has a friend who cares for him. It is a cruel life if you must live all alone in the world."

In the next room, Victor tosses in his troubled sleep. He dreams he has returned to his father's home in Geneva. Elizabeth rushes down the stone steps of Frankenstein Castle to meet him. He embraces her, places his lips over hers—Suddenly, her face changes. Her lips shrivel and turn black. The skin over her cheekbones withers and flakes away. Graveyard worms crawl in the folds of her dress.

"No! No! Lizzie! What have I done?" Victor cries in his sleep.

Henry hurries to his side. He shakes Victor gently. "It was just a bad dream, Victor. Do you understand? It was only a dream."

Victor stares hard at his friend. "Henry? When did you come? Why are you here?"

"Your father sent me. You are ill, Victor. You need to rest."

"Elizabeth? Henry, where is Lizzie?"

"She is home with your father in Geneva. She sends you her love." On the bed table is a picture of Elizabeth. Henry reaches for it and stares at the dark-eyed beauty. He smiles. "You are a lucky fellow, Victor. I don't mind telling you that I'd marry Lizzie in a minute, but she waits only for you."

Victor turns away from the image. "Where are my papers? My books?"

"Everything was destroyed in the fire."

Now Victor remembers . . . the shriveled lips, the gaping mouth struggling to breathe, the electrical current that jolted the carcass. Victor grips Henry's arm fiercely. "You are certain that everything was destroyed? *Everything?*"

"Quite certain," Henry answers. "I'm so sorry, Victor. Now I insist, you must rest. You must try to sleep."

Victor falls back against his pillows. He closes his eyes. Henry snuffs out the candle and quietly steps from the room. And yet, Victor is not quite alone. Outside the window's black glass, eyes swollen and red from smoke and fire keep watch. They are the eyes of a creature, once dead but now alive because of Frankenstein's science. In Greek mythology Prometheus gave the gift of fire to the world. From Frankenstein's fire has come a new Prometheus, and one day he will destroy his creator.

PART 2

WHAT IS THE FUTURE

o o o

Today, the future is alien indeed.

FUTURE TENSE

BY ROBERT LIPSYTE

◻ ◻ ◻

**Was Gary writing himself
into a crazed state? Or was his
imagination coming true?**

Gary couldn't wait for tenth grade to start so
he could strut his sentences, parade his paragraphs,
and renew his reputation as the top creative writer
in school. At the opening assembly, he felt on edge,
psyched, like a boxer before the first bell. He leaned
forward as Dr. Proctor, the principal, introduced
two new staff members.

Gary wasn't particularly interested in the new
vice-principal, Ms. Jones. Gary had never had discipline problems—he'd never even had to stay
after school. But his head tilted alertly as Dr.
Proctor introduced the new honors English
teacher, Mr. Smith. Here was the person he'd have
to impress.

Gary studied Mr. Smith. The man was hard to describe. He looked as though he'd been manufactured to fit his name. Average height, brownish hair, pale white skin, medium build, middle age. He was the sort of person you began to forget the minute you met him. Even his clothes had no special style. They merely covered his body.

Mr. Smith was . . . just there.

Gary was studying the newcomer so intently that he didn't hear Dr. Proctor call him up to the stage to receive an award from last term. Jim Baggs jabbed an elbow into his ribs and said, "Get up there, dude."

Dr. Proctor shook Gary's hand and gave him the County Medal for Best Composition. While Dr. Proctor was giving Jim Baggs the County Trophy for Best All-Around Athlete, Gary glanced over his shoulder to see if Mr. Smith looked impressed. But he couldn't find the new teacher. Gary wondered if Mr. Smith was so ordinary that he became invisible when no one was talking about him.

On the way home, Dani Belzer, the prettiest poet in school, asked Gary, "What did you think of our new Mr. Wordsmith?"

"If he were a color, he'd be beige," said Gary. "If he were a taste, he'd be water. If he were a sound, he'd be a low hum."

"Fancy, empty words," sneered Mike Chung, ace reporter on the school paper. "All you've told me is that you've got nothing to tell me."

Dani quickly stepped between them. "What did you think of the first assignment?"

"Describe a typical day at school," said Gary, trying unsuccessfully to mimic Mr. Smith's bland voice. "That's about as exciting as instant mashed potatoes."

"A real artist," said Dani, "accepts the ordinary as a challenge."

                    0   0   0

That night, hunched over his humming computer, Gary wrote a description of a typical day at school from the viewpoint of a new teacher. Someone who was seeing everything for the first time, who took nothing for granted. Gary described the shredded edges of the limp flag outside the dented front door, the worn flooring where generations of kids had nervously paced outside the principal's office, the nauseating cigarette smoke seeping from the lavatories.

And then, in the last line, he gave the composition that extra twist, the little kicker on which his reputation rested. He wrote:

*The new teacher's beady little eyes missed
nothing, for they were the optical recorders
of an alien creature who had come to Earth
to gather information.*

The next morning, when Mr. Smith asked for a vol-
unteer to read aloud, Gary was on his feet and moving toward the front of the classroom before Mike
Chung could get his hand out of his pocket.

The class loved Gary's composition. Students
laughed and stamped their feet. Mike shrugged,
which meant he couldn't think of any criticism, and
Dani flashed thumbs up. Best of all, Jim Baggs
shouldered Gary against the blackboard after class
and said, "Awesome tale, dude."

Gary felt good until he got his composition
back. Along one margin, in a perfect script, Mr.
Smith had written: *You can do better.*

"How would he know?" Gary complained on
the way home.

"You should be grateful," said Dani. "He's
pushing you to the furthest limits of your talent."

"Which may be nearer than you think," snick-
ered Mike.

Gary rewrote his composition—expanded it,
complicated it, thickened it. Not only was this new

teacher an alien, he was also part of an extraterrestrial conspiracy to take over Earth. Gary's final sentences were:

> *Every iota of information and fragment of fact sucked up by those vacuuming eyes was beamed directly to a computer circling the planet. The data would eventually become a program that would control the mind of every school kid on Earth.*

Gary showed the new draft to Dani before class. Gary stood on tiptoe so he could read over her shoulder. Sometimes he wished she were shorter, but mostly he wished he were taller.

"What do you think?"

"The assignment was to describe a typical day," said Dani. "This is off the wall."

He snatched the papers back. "Creative writing means creating." He walked away, hurt and angry. He thought: *If she doesn't like my compositions, how can I ever get her to like me?*

That morning, Mike Chung read his own composition aloud to the class. He described a typical day through the eyes of a student in a wheelchair. Everything most students take for granted was an obstacle—the bathroom door too heavy to open, the gym ramps too steep to climb, the light switch too high on the wall. The class applauded, and Mr. Smith nodded approvingly. Even Gary had to admit it was really good—if you considered plain-fact journalism to be creative writing, that is.

Gary's rewrite came back the next day. It was marked: *Improving. Try again.*

o   o   o

On Saturday, he locked himself in his room after breakfast and rewrote the rewrite. He carefully selected his nouns and verbs and adjectives. He polished and arranged them in sentences the way a jeweler strings pearls. He felt good as he wrote, as the computer hummed and the cursor blinked approval. He thought: *Every champion knows that as hard as it is to get to the top, it's even harder to stay up there.*

Gary's mother knocked on his door around noon. When he let her in, she said, "It's a beautiful day."

"Big project," he mumbled. He wanted to avoid a distracting conversation.

She smiled. "If you spend too much time in your room, you'll turn into a mushroom."

He wasn't listening. "Thanks. Anything's OK. Don't forget the mayonnaise." Gary wrote:

The alien's probes trembled as it read the student's composition. Could that skinny, glasses-wearing Earthling really suspect its extraterrestrial identity? Or was his composition merely coincidence—the result of a creative mushroom in a brilliant young mind?

o   o   o

Before Gary turned in his composition Monday morning, he showed it to Mike Chung. He should have known better.

"You're trying too hard," chortled Mike. "Truth is stronger than fiction."

Gary flinched at that. It hurt. It might be true. But he couldn't let his competition know he had scored. "You journalists are stuck in the present and in the past," growled Gary. "Imagination prepares us for what's going to happen."

Dani read her composition aloud to the class. It described a typical day from the perspective of a louse choosing a head of hair to nest in. The louse moved from the thicket of a varsity crew cut to the matted jungle of a sagging perm to a straight, sleek blond cascade.

The class cheered, and Mr. Smith smiled. Gary felt a twinge of jealousy. Dani and Mike were coming on. There wasn't room for more than one at the top.

In the hallway, Gary said to Dani, "And you called *my* composition off the wall."

Mike jumped in. "There's a big difference between an imaginative comparison and hack science fiction."

Gary felt choked by a lump in his throat. He hurried away.

Mr. Smith handed back Gary's composition the next day. It was marked: *See me after school.*

o o o

Gary was nervous all day. What was there to talk about? Maybe Mr. Smith hated science fiction. One of those traditional English teachers. Didn't understand that science fiction could be literature. *Maybe I can educate him,* thought Gary.

When Gary arrived at the English office, Mr. Smith seemed nervous too. He kept folding and unfolding Gary's composition. "Where do you get such ideas?" he asked in his monotone voice.

Gary shrugged. "They just come to me."

"Alien teachers. Taking over the minds of schoolchildren." Mr. Smith's empty eyes were blinking. "What made you think of that?"

"I've always had this vivid imagination."

"If you're sure it's just your imagination." Mr. Smith looked relieved. "I guess everything will work out." He handed back Gary's composition. "No more fantasy, Gary. Reality. That's your assignment. Write about only what you know."

Outside school, Gary ran into Jim Baggs, who looked surprised to see him. "Don't tell me you had to stay after school, dude."

"I had to see Mr. Smith about my composition. He didn't like it. Told me to stick to reality."

"Don't listen." Jim Baggs bodychecked Gary into the schoolyard fence. "Dude, you got to be yourself."

Gary ran all the way home and locked himself in his room. He felt feverish with creativity. Dude, you got to be yourself. It doesn't matter what your so-called friends say or your English teacher. You've got to play your own king of game, write your own kind of stories.

The words flowed from Gary's mind and through his fingers and out of the machine and onto sheets of paper. He wrote and rewrote until he felt the words were exactly right.

With great effort, the alien shut down the electrical panic impulses coursing through its sys-

*tem and turned on Logical Overdrive. There
were two possibilities:
1. This high school boy was exactly what he
appeared to be—a brilliant, imaginative,
best-selling author and screen-writer-to-be.
2. The boy had somehow stumbled onto the
secret plan, and he would either have to be
enlisted into the conspiracy or be erased from
the face of the planet.*

o o o

First thing in the morning, Gary turned in his new
rewrite to Mr. Smith. Half an hour later, Mr. Smith
called Gary out of Spanish class. There was no expression on his everyday, average face. He said, "I'm
going to need some help with you."

A cold sweat broke out over Gary's body as Mr.
Smith grabbed his arm and led him to the new vice-
principal. She read the composition while they
waited. Gary took a good look at her for the first
time. Ms. Jones was . . . just there. She looked as
though she'd been manufactured to fit her name.
Average. Standard. Typical. Gary's cold sweat turned
to goose pimples.

How could he have missed the clues? Smith
and Jones were aliens! He had stumbled on their
secret, and now they'd have to deal with him.

He blurted, "Are you going to enlist me or erase me?"

Ms. Jones ignored him. "In my opinion, Mr. Smith, you are overreacting. This sort of non-sense"—she waved Gary's composition—"is the response of an adolescent overstimulated by all the junky music, TV, and movies around these days. Nothing for us to worry about."

"If you're sure, Ms. Jones," said Mr. Smith. He didn't sound sure.

The vice-principal looked at Gary for the first time. There was no expression in her eyes. Her voice was flat. "You'd better get off this science fiction kick," she said, "if you know what's good for you."

"I'll never tell another human being, I swear!" Gary babbled.

"What are you talking about?" asked Ms. Jones.

"Your secret is safe with me," Gary lied. He thought, *If I can just get away from them. Alert the authorities. Save the planet.*

"You see," said Ms. Jones, "you're writing yourself into a crazed state."

"You're beginning to believe your own fantasies," said Mr. Smith.

"I'm not going to do anything this time," said Ms. Jones, "but you must promise to write about only what you know."

"Or I'll have to fail you," said Mr. Smith.

"For your own good," said Ms. Jones. She paused. "Writing can be very dangerous."

"Especially for writers," said Mr. Smith as he stared into Gary's eyes, "who write about things they shouldn't."

"Absolutely," said Gary, "positively, no question about it. Only what I know." He backed out the door, nodding his head, thinking, *Just a few more steps and I'm OK. I hope these aliens can't read minds.*

◦　◦　◦

Jim Baggs was practicing head fakes in the hallway. He slammed Gary into the wall with a hip block. "How's it going, dude?" he asked, helping Gary up.

"Aliens," gasped Gary. "Told me no more science fiction."

"They can't treat a star writer like that," said Jim. "See what the head honcho's got to say." He grabbed Gary's wrist and dragged him to the principal's office.

"What can I do for you, boys?" boomed Dr. Proctor.

"They're messing with his moves, Doc," said Jim Baggs. "You got to let the aces run their races."

"Thank you, James." Dr. Proctor popped his forefinger at the door. "I'll handle this."

"You're home free, dude," said Jim, whacking Gary across the shoulder blades as he left.

"From the beginning," ordered Dr. Proctor. He nodded sympathetically as Gary told the entire story—from the opening assembly to the meeting with Dr. Smith and Ms. Jones. When Gary was finished, Dr. Proctor took the papers from Gary's hand. He shook his head as he read Gary's latest rewrite.

"You really have a way with words, Gary. I should have sensed you were on to something."

Gary's stomach flipped. "You really think there could be aliens trying to take over Earth?"

"Of course," Dr. Proctor said matter-of-factly. "Earth is the ripest plum in this galaxy."

Gary wasn't sure if he should feel relieved that he wasn't crazy or be scared out of his mind. He took a deep breath to control the quaver in his voice and said, "I spotted Smith and Jones right away. They look like they were manufactured to fit their names. Obviously humanoids. Panicked as soon as they knew I was onto them."

Dr. Proctor chuckled and shook his head. "No self-respecting civilization would send those two stiffs to Earth."

"They're not aliens?" Gary felt relieved and disappointed at the same time.

"I checked them out myself," said Dr. Proctor. "Just two average, dull, humdrum human beings."

"So why'd you hire them?"

Dr. Proctor laughed. "Because they'd never spot an alien. No imagination, no creativity. That's why I got rid of the last vice-principal and the last honors English teacher. They were giving me odd little glances when they thought I wasn't looking. After ten years on your planet, I've learned to smell trouble."

Gary's spine turned to water and dripped down the back of his legs. "You . . . you're . . . an alien?"

"Great composition," said Dr. Proctor, waving Gary's papers. "Grammatical, vividly written, and totally accurate."

"It's just a composition," babbled Gary. "Made the whole thing up. Imagination, you know."

Dr. Proctor removed the face of his wristwatch and began tapping tiny buttons. "Always liked writers. I majored in your planet's literature. Writers are the keepers of the past and the hope of the future. Too bad they cause so much trouble in the present."

"I won't tell anyone," cried Gary. "Your secret is safe with me." He began backing slowly toward the door.

Dr. Proctor shook his head. "How can writers keep secrets, Gary? It's their nature to share their creations with the world." He tapped three times and froze Gary in place, one foot raised to step out the door.

"But it was only a composition," screamed Gary as his body faded and disappeared before his eyes.

"And I can't wait to hear what the folks back home say when you read it to them," said Dr. Proctor.

"I made it all up!" Gary had the sensation of rocketing upward. "I made up the whole . . ."

REASON

BY ISAAC ASIMOV

o   o   o

**The space station had two problems—
a solar storm that threatened to destroy
Earth and . . . Cutie.**

Gregory Powell tugged nervously at the end
of his mustache and spoke with care. "One week
ago Donovan and I put you together."

Except for the soft purring of the Energy
Beamer somewhere far below, the officer's room of
Solar Station 5 was quiet. Robot QT-1 sat unmov-
ing, his photoelectric eyes fixed on the human.

Powell felt uneasy. These robots had weird
brains. Their circuits were programmed to rule out
anything that might lead to anger or hate. Even so,
the QT models were new, and this was the first QT.
Anything could happen.

Finally the robot spoke in its metallic voice.
"Do you realize what you are saying, Powell?"

"*Something* made you, Cutie," Powell replied. "You admit yourself that your memory goes blank when it tries to reach back more than a week. I'm telling you why. Donovan and I put you together from parts shipped to us."

QT's eyes glowed redder. "It strikes me that there should be a better explanation than that. For *you* to make *me* seems most unlikely."

Powell laughed nervously. "Why?"

"Call it a feeling I have. But I intend to reason it out. A chain of logical thought can end only with the truth."

Powell felt a sudden sympathy for this strange machine. It wasn't at all like the ordinary robot, busily following its present programs.

"Cutie," he said, "you're the first robot that's ever wondered about its own existence—and the first that's really smart enough to understand the world outside. Here, come with me."

Moving smoothly, the robot followed Powell to a section of glass. Beyond was black space speckled with stars.

"What do you think you are looking at?" asked Powell.

QT didn't hesitate. "Exactly what it seems—a vast emptiness, reaching out trillions of miles. The dots are huge masses of energy-filled matter."

"They're called stars," Powell interrupted. "We have our own star called the sun. This space station takes the energy from the sun and changes it to a powerful beam. We send the beam down to our planet, where a lot of beings like me live. We call our planet Earth. And in about two weeks Donovan and I will be back there with our friends."

QT started to hum softly. Then the humming stopped. "Where do I come in, Powell? You haven't explained *my* existence."

Powell put his hand on QT's shoulder. "That's simple. We created you to run this space station. You're the highest type of robot we ever made. We created you to serve us."

Powell started to return to the table but stopped in the red glow of the robot's eyes. "Do you expect me to believe such a wild theory?" QT asked.

Powell's face turned red. "It's not a theory. It's a fact."

QT's metallic voice sounded grim. "Planets with humans on them! Sorry, Powell, but I don't believe it. I'll reason this out for myself. Good-bye."

QT turned and walked silently from the room, brushing past Michael Donovan, who was just entering. Donovan shot a puzzled glance at Powell. "What was that walking junkyard talking about? What doesn't he believe?"

Powell was tugging his mustache again. "He doesn't believe that we made him or that Earth exists."

"You mean we've got a crazy robot on our hands?"

"You tell me. He says he has to figure it out for himself."

Donovan dropped into a chair and pulled a paperback mystery from his jacket. "That robot gives me the willies anyway—too darn curious."

Powell sighed. "I guess we're stuck with a monster of our own making."

◦   ◦   ◦

Mike Donovan scowled from behind a huge chicken sandwich as QT knocked gently and entered. "Is Powell here?" the robot asked.

Donovan's voice was muffled from chewing. "He's gathering data on the sun's radiation."

At that moment Powell entered. He spread out sheets of paper and began doing calculations. Finally he looked up. "Oh, hello, Cutie, I thought you were supervising work on a drive bar."

"It's done," said the robot quietly, "and so I've come to have a talk with the two of you."

"Oh?" Powell looked worried.

"Yes," said QT calmly. "I have spent the last two days in thought and have reached my own answer."

Powell's jaw set stubbornly. "I told you already how things are. We made you."

The robot spread his strong hands. "I accept nothing on your say-so. A theory must be backed by reason, or it is worthless. And it is not logical to suppose that you made me."

"And why is that?" Donovan asked.

QT laughed a very inhuman laugh. "I say this in no spirit of scorn, but look at you. The material you are made of is soft and flabby. You lack endurance and strength." QT pointed to Donovan's sandwich and then continued. "Your fuel comes from once-living matter, and you convert it to energy at a very inefficient rate. Every 16 hours or so, you pass into a coma. The least change in temperature, air pressure, or radiation slows you down. We must face facts, gentlemen. You are *makeshift*."

Donovan clenched his fists.

"I, on the other hand, am a finished product. I use electrical energy with almost 100 percent efficiency. I am composed of strong metal. I am always conscious. I can easily stand extremes of environment. Now, it is obvious that no being can create another being superior to itself. Therefore, your theory is wrong."

Now Donovan sprang to his feet. "All right, you conceited hunk of iron, if we didn't make you, who did?"

QT nodded gravely. "Very good, Donovan. That is indeed the next question. Clearly, my creator must be more powerful than myself. So there is just one possibility."

The humans from Earth looked blank, and QT continued. "What is the center of activity in the station? What do we all serve?"

Donovan turned a startled glance upon his companion. "I'll bet this tin-plated screwball is talking about the Energy Beamer itself."

"Is that right, Cutie?" grinned Powell.

"I am talking about the Master," came the cold, sharp reply.

Donovan broke into a roar of laughter, and Powell himself had to hide a giggle.

QT's eyes flashed red. "I don't wonder that you refuse to believe, but I shall tell you the truth anyway."

"Go ahead, Cutie," said Donovan. "Give us another laugh."

"The Master created humans first as the lowest type, most easily formed. Then the Master created robots, the next higher step. Finally the Master created me, the highest type of all. The Master has decided to replace you with me. From now on, *I* serve the Master—not you."

"You'll do nothing of the sort," said Powell sharply. "You will follow our orders until we are sure that you can run the Beamer. Get that? The *Beamer*—not the Master. If you don't obey us, you will be taken apart. And now you may leave."

QT left without another word. Donovan leaned back in his chair and shoved thick fingers through his hair.

"There's going to be trouble with that robot. It's pure nuts."

o   o   o

Powell stood in the control room holding a bundle of papers. "What do you think of these figures?" he said to Donovan.

Donovan looked at them and whistled. "The old sun is really getting stirred up. It could throw an electrical storm right at us."

"Right," was Powell's worried response. "And that storm could make the beam jump like a flea with an itch." Powell sighed. If the beam went out of focus and missed the receiving station on Earth, it could blast millions of square miles into smoking ruins.

Now there were two problems on Solar Space Station 5—the solar storm . . . and Cutie.

"I wonder what Cutie's up to," Powell said. "Could you check on him, Mike?"

"Sure," said Donovan, heading for the elevator. It slid downward and opened on a narrow catwalk above a huge room. Down below, the Beamer trapped energy from the sun and sent that energy to Earth. Donovan could see QT watching closely as a team of robots worked the controls.

And then Donovan stiffened. The robots, dwarfed by the mighty Beamer, lined up before it. Their heads bowed at a stiff angle as QT walked down the line. Fifteen seconds passed and then, with a clank, they fell to their knees.

Donovan yelled and ran down the narrow staircase. "What's going on here, you brainless lumps?" he shouted. "Come on, get busy with the Beamer. Now!"

Not a robot moved.

Donovan shoved hard against the nearest one. "Stand up!" he roared.

Slowly the robot obeyed, its electric eyes gleaming.

"There is no Master but the Master," it said, "and QT-1 is his prophet."

"I fear," QT explained, "that my friends now obey one higher than you."

Donovan scowled. "They'd better not. You get out of here, Cutie. I'll settle with you later and with these crazy gadgets now."

QT shook his heavy head. "I'm sorry, but you don't understand. I have preached the truth to my friends, and they have seen the light. I am the Master's prophet."

"Is that so? Let me tell you something, my brass baboon," Donovan sputtered angrily. "There is no Master, and no prophet, and no question about who's boss around here. Now get out!"

QT moved toward Donovan, who felt a quick surge of fear. A robot *could not feel* anger. And yet . . .

"I am sorry, Donovan," said QT quietly, "but you can no longer stay here. I have barred you and Powell from any work with the Master."

QT gestured, and two robots pinned Donovan's arms to his side. He had time for one startled gasp as he was lifted from the floor and carried swiftly upstairs.

o   o   o

Gregory Powell raced up and down the officer's room, fists clenched. He cast a look of furious frustration at the closed door and at Donovan.

"Why the devil did you have to get Cutie stirred up?"

Mike Donovan, sunk deep in a chair, uttered angrily, "What did you expect me to do, take orders from something I built myself?"

"No," came back the sour reply, "but here you are in the officer's room with two robots guarding the door. I don't exactly call that being in charge."

Donovan snarled. "Wait till we get home. Someone's going to pay for designing the mixed-up metal moron."

"We may not want to go home," Powell replied. "That energy storm is heading straight across the Earth's beam."

Donovan paled, "Oh, no!"

"Right. And with only Cutie at the controls, Heaven help Earth—and us."

Donovan wrenched the door open wildly and started through—only to bang hard against a steel arm.

The robot stared calmly at the panting, struggling human. QT appeared and motioned the guardian robots away. He entered the officer's room and closed the door gently.

Donovan whirled on QT in breathless indignation. "You won't get away with this."

"Please don't be annoyed," said the robot mildly. One arm shot out and draped around Powell's shoulder. The other grasped Donovan's wrist and pulled him closer.

"I like you two. I really do. You're weak creatures with small brains, but I feel affection for you. Now that the Master has decided to phase you out, I want your last days to be happy. Just remain in this room, and all your needs will be provided."

"Did you hear that?" yelled Donovan. "He's treating us like pets. Do something, Greg."

Powell tugged furiously at his mustache. "Do what? If you can think of anything, let me know."

"I'll send you food," said QT pleasantly.

A groan was the only answer as the robot left.

"Greg," Donovan whispered, "this calls for a plan. We have to get him when he isn't expecting it and short-circuit him. Some nitric acid in his joints would—"

"Don't be a dope, Mike. Do you suppose he's going to let us near him with acid in our hands. And even if we stopped him, the other robots would take us apart. We've built ourselves a monster—that's what we've done."

Donovan started pacing back and forth. "We can't just sit here and let Earth suffer the effects of that storm." Donovan was half in tears. "It's due *tomorrow*."

"I know," said Powell bitterly, "but there's nothing else we can do."

◊　　◊　　◊

The storm arrived ahead of schedule. Donovan's finger shook as he pointed at the glass, and Powell tugged desperately at his mustache.

It *was* a beautiful sight. The stream of electrons striking the energy beam gave a dancing light show. But it was also a deadly sight. Life as they had known it on Earth was being destroyed. And a crazy robot, unconcerned with anything but the Master, was at the controls.

Hours passed. Powell and Donovan watched the storm in fascinated silence. And then the light show dimmed and went out. The storm had ended.

Powell's voice was flat. "It's over."

Then QT was there. His voice was low. "You don't look at all well, and I'm afraid that your end is drawing near. Trust in the Master, and all will be well."

"Thanks," said Powell glumly. Much of Earth had been wiped out, and that dumb robot wouldn't shut up about the Master.

QT spoke again, almost as if he were trying to be friendly. "Would you like to see some of today's readings?"

Well, *why not?* thought Powell. He accepted the sheets held out to him and gazed at them blankly. Suddenly his blurred sight focused on a red line that wobbled across the papers.

Powell jumped to his feet, still staring. "Mike, Mike!" He was shaking Donovan madly. "Cutie held the beam steady!"

Donovan rose from the chair where he had slumped. And he, too, stared with amazed eyes at the record before him.

QT broke in. "What's wrong?"

"You kept the beam aimed sharply at the receiving station."

"What receiving station?"

"On Earth. The one on Earth," babbled Powell. "You kept it in focus."

QT was annoyed. "It is impossible to be nice to you two. Always that meaningless talk about Earth. I merely kept all the dials in balance as the Master wills it."

Gathering the scattered papers together, QT turned on his heels and walked out. Donovan stared after him in amazement, then turned to Powell. "Well, now what?"

Powell was very tired but also very happy. "Nothing. He's just shown us he can run the station perfectly."

"But he's still yapping about the Master. We can't let him continue that nitwit stuff."

Powell grinned. "Why not? Can he *handle* the station?"

"Yes, but—"

"Then what's the difference *what* he believes in?"

Powell spread his arms outward with a big smile and tumbled backward onto his bed. He was asleep.

0   0   0

Some hours later, Powell struggled into his space jacket, ready to head for Earth. "It would be a simple job," he was telling Donovan. "You bring in new QT models one by one and let them learn the . . . uh . . . cult of the Master from the Prophet himself. Then you switch them to another station. We could have two QT's per—"

Donovan put on his helmet and scowled. "I won't feel right until I land on Earth and know it's really there."

The door opened as Donovan spoke, and QT entered. With a grunt of disgust, Donovan clicked his helmet shut and turned his back. The robot approached softly, and sorrow was in his voice. "You are going?"

Powell nodded. "There will be others in our place."

QT sighed, with the sound of wind humming through closely spaced wires. "Your term of service is over and you are about to be phased out. I expected it, but—well, the Master's wish be done!"

His tone stung Powell. "Save the sympathy, Cutie. We're heading for the Earth, not death."

"It is best that you think so," QT sighed again. "I see the wisdom of the illusion now. I would not attempt to shake your faith even if I could."

QT left, the picture of gentle misery. Powell shook his head and motioned to Donovan. They headed for the airlock.

The relief ship was on the outer landing, and Ivan Petrov, leader of the oncoming relief team, greeted them coldly. Donovan passed into the pilot room, but Powell lingered. "How's Earth?" he asked.

It was the usual question, and Petrov gave the usual answer. "Still spinning." His thick eyebrows drew close together. "I hope you Americans haven't messed up anything. Have you trained the new robot to follow orders exactly?"

Powell paused, looking at this arrogant Russian with the superior sneer. Suddenly he felt a glow of pure gladness. "The robot is pretty good," Powell said slowly, "and he certainly knows who his master is."

"Excellent," said Petrov, "I was afraid you Americans might have botched the job of training QT-1. It had better follow my orders precisely, or I won't let it near the controls."

Powell said no more. Whistling happily, he went into the relief ship. Petrov would be on the space station with Cutie for several weeks—with no way to get off. *Should be quite a show*, Powell thought as the airlock closed behind him.

APRIL 2000:
THE THIRD EXPEDITION

FROM *THE MARTIAN CHRONICLES* BY RAY BRADBURY

□   □   □

**They never expected the Martians
to look so . . . familiar.**

The ship came down from space. It came from
the stars and the black velocities, and the shining
movements, and the silent gulfs of space. It was a
new ship; it had fire in its body and men in its metal
cells, and it moved with a clean silence, fiery and
warm. In it were seventeen men, including a captain. The crowd at the Ohio field had shouted and
waved their hands up into the sunlight, and the
rocket had bloomed out great flowers of heat and
color and run away into space on the *third* voyage
to Mars!

Now it was decelerating with metal efficiency
in the upper Martian atmospheres. It was still a
thing of beauty and strength. It had moved in the

midnight waters of space like a pale sea leviathan; it had passed the ancient moon and thrown itself onward into one nothingness following another. The men within it had been battered, thrown about, sickened, made well again, each in his turn. One man had died, but now the remaining sixteen, with their eyes clear in their heads and their faces pressed to the thick glass ports, watched Mars swing up under them.

"Mars!" cried   or Lustig.

"Good old M   amuel Hinkston, archaeologist.

"Well," said C   Black.

The rock   of green grass. Outside, upon   ood   iron deer. Farther up on the g   ood a tall brown Victorian house, quiet in the sunlight, all covered with scrolls and rococo, its windows made of blue and pink and yellow and green colored glass. Upon the porch were hairy geraniums and an old swing which was hooked into the porch ceiling and which now swung back and forth, back and forth, in a little breeze. At the summit of the house was a cupola with diamond leaded-glass windows and a dunce-cap roof! Through the front window you could see a piece of music titled "Beautiful Ohio" sitting on the music rest.

Around the rocket in four directions spread the little town, green and motionless in the Martian spring. There were white houses and red brick ones, and tall elm trees blowing in the wind, and tall maples and horse chestnuts. And church steeples with golden bells silent in them.

The rocket men looked out and saw this. Then they looked at one another and then they looked out again. They held to each other's elbows, suddenly unable to br   faces grew pale.

"I'll be   Lustig, rubbing his face with   be damned."

"It just c   Hinkston.

"Lord," said C.   Black.

There was a call from the chemist. "Sir, the atmosphere is thin for breathing. But there's enough oxygen. It's safe."

"Then we'll go out," said Lustig.

"Hold on," said Captain John Black. "How do we know what this is?"

"It's a small town with thin but breathable air in it, sir."

"And it's a small town the like of Earth towns," said Hinkston, the archaeologist. "Incredible. It can't be, but it *is*."

Captain John Black looked at him idly. "Do you think that the civilizations of two planets can progress at the same rate and evolve in the same way, Hinkston?"

"I wouldn't have thought so, sir."

Captain Black stood by the port. "Look out there. The geraniums. A specialized plant. That specific variety has only been known on Earth for fifty years. Think of the thousands of years it takes to evolve plants. Then tell me if it is logical that the Martians should have: one, leaded-glass windows; two, cupolas; three, porch swings; four, an instrument that looks like a piano and probably *is* a piano; and five, if you look closely through this telescopic lens here, is it logical that a Martian composer would have published a piece of music titled, strangely enough, 'Beautiful Ohio'? all of which means that we have an Ohio River on Mars!"

"Captain Williams, of course!" cried Hinkston.

"What?"

"Captain Williams and his crew of three men! Or Nathaniel York and his partner. That would explain it!"

"That would explain absolutely nothing. As far as we've been able to figure, the York expedition exploded the day it reached Mars, killing York and his partner. As for Williams and his three men, their ship exploded the second day after their arrival. At least the pulsations from their radios ceased at that time so we figure that if the men were alive after that they'd have contacted us. And anyway, the York expedition was only a year ago, while Captain Williams and his men landed here some time during August. Theorizing that they are still alive, could they, even with the help of a brilliant Martian race, have built such a town as this and *aged* it in so short a time? Look at that town out there; why, it's been standing here for the last seventy years. Look at the wood on the porch newel; look at the trees, a century old, all of them! No, this isn't York's work or Williams'. It's something else. I don't like it. And I'm not leaving the ship until I know what it is."

"For that matter," said Lustig, nodding, "Williams and his men, as well as York, landed on the *opposite* side of Mars. We were very careful to land on *this* side."

"An excellent point. Just in case a hostile local tribe of Martians killed off York and Williams, we have instructions to land in a further region, to forestall a recurrence of such a disaster. So here we are, as far as we know, in a land that Williams and York never saw."

"Damn it," said Hinkston. "I want to get out into this town, sir, with your permission. It may be there *are* similar thought patterns, civilization graphs on every planet in our sun system. We may be on the threshold of the greatest psychological and metaphysical discovery of our age!"

"I'm willing to wait a moment," said Captain John Black.

"It may be, sir, that we're looking upon a phenomenon that, for the first time, would absolutely prove the existence of God, sir."

"There are many people who are of good faith without such proof, Mr. Hinkston."

"I'm one myself, sir. But certainly a town like this could not occur without divine intervention. The *detail*. It fills me with such feelings that I don't know whether to laugh or cry."

"Do neither, then, until we know what we're up against."

"Up against?" Lustig broke in. "Against nothing, Captain. It's a good, quiet green town, a lot like the old-fashioned one I was born in. I like the looks of it."

"When were you born, Lustig?" the captain asked.

"Nineteen-fifty, sir."

"And you, Hinkston?"

"Nineteen fifty-five, sir. Grinnell, Iowa. And this looks like home to me."

"Hinkston, Lustig, I could be either of your fathers. I'm just eighty years old. Born in 1920 in Illinois, and through the grace of God and a science that, in the last fifty years, knew how to make *some* old men young again, here I am on Mars, not any more tired than the rest of you, but infinitely more suspicious. This town out here looks very peaceful and cool, and so much like Green Bluff, Illinois, that it frightens me. It's too *much* like Green Bluff." He turned to the radioman. "Radio Earth. Tell them we've landed. That's all. Tell them we'll radio a full report tomorrow."

"Yes, sir."

Captain Black looked out the rocket port with his face that should have been the face of a man eighty but seemed like the face of a man in his fortieth year. "Tell you what we'll do, Lustig; you and I and Hinkston will look the town over. The other men will stay aboard. If anything happens they can get the hell out. A loss of three men's better than a whole ship. If something bad happens, our crew can warn the next rocket. That's Captain Wilder's rocket, I think, due to be ready to take off next Christmas. If there's something hostile about Mars we certainly want the next rocket to be well armed."

"So are we. We've got a regular arsenal with us."

"Tell the men to stand by the guns then. Come on, Lustig, Hinkston."

The three men walked together down through the levels of the ship.

◦   ◦   ◦

It was a beautiful spring day. A robin sat on a blossoming apple tree and sang continuously. Showers of petal snow sifted down when the wind touched the green branches, and the blossom scent drifted upon the air. Somewhere in the town someone was playing the piano and the music came and went, came and went, softly, drowsily. The song was "Beautiful Dreamer." Somewhere else a phonograph, scratchy and faded, was hissing out a record of "Roamin' in the Gloamin'," sung by Harry Lauder.

The three men stood outside the ship. They sucked and gasped at the thin, thin air and moved slowly so as not to tire themselves.

Now the phonograph record being played was:
"Oh give me a June night
The moonlight and you . . ."

Lustig began to tremble. Samuel Hinkston did likewise.

The sky was serene and quiet, and somewhere a stream of water ran through the cool caverns and tree shadings of a ravine. Somewhere a horse and wagon trotted and rolled by, bumping.

"Sir," said Samuel Hinkston, "it must be, it *has* to be, that rocket travel to Mars began in the years before the First World War!"

"No."

"How else can you explain these houses, the iron deer, the pianos, the music?" Hinkston took the captain's elbow persuasively and looked into the captain's face. "Say that there were people in the year 1905 who hated war and got together with some scientists in secret and built a rocket and came out here to Mars—"

"No, no, Hinkston."

"Why not? The world was a different world in 1905; they could have kept it a secret much more easily."

"But a complex thing like a rocket, no, you couldn't keep it secret."

"And they came up here to live and naturally the houses they built were similar to Earth houses because they brought the culture with them."

"And they've lived here all these years?" said the captain.

"In peace and quiet, yes. Maybe they made a few trips, enough to bring enough people here for one small town, and then stopped for fear of being discovered. That's why this town seems so old-fashioned. I don't see a thing, myself, older than the year 1927, do you? Or maybe, sir, rocket travel is older than we think. Perhaps it started in some part of the world centuries ago and was kept secret by the small number of men who came to Mars with only occasional visits to Earth over the centuries."

"You make it sound almost reasonable."

"It has to be. We've the proof here before us; all we have to do is find some people and verify it."

Their boots were deadened of all sound in the thick green grass. It smelled from a fresh mowing. In spite of himself, Captain John Black felt a great peace come over him. It had been thirty years since he had been in a small town, and the buzzing of spring bees on the air lulled and quieted him, and the fresh look of things was a balm to the soul.

They set foot upon the porch. Hollow echoes sounded from under the boards as they walked to the screen door. Inside they could see a bead curtain hung across the hall entry, and a crystal chandelier and a Maxfield Parrish painting framed on one wall over a comfortable Morris chair. The house smelled old, and of the attic, and infinitely comfortable. You could hear the tinkle of ice in a lemonade pitcher. In a distant kitchen, because of the heat of the day, someone was preparing a cold lunch. Someone was humming under her breath, high and sweet.

Captain John Black rang the bell.

◦   ◦   ◦

Footsteps, dainty and thin, came along the hall, and a kind-faced lady of some forty years, dressed in a sort of dress you might expect in the year 1909, peered out at them.

"Can I help you?" she asked.

"Beg your pardon," said Captain Black uncertainly. "But we're looking for—that is, could you help us—" He stopped. She looked out at him with dark, wondering eyes.

"If you're selling something—" she began.

"No, wait!" he cried. "What town is this?"

She looked him up and down. "What do you mean, what town is it? How could you be in a town and not know the name?"

The captain looked as if he wanted to go sit under a shady apple tree. "We're strangers here. We want to know how this town got here and how you got here."

"Are you census takers?"

"No."

"Everyone knows," she said, "this town was built in 1868. Is this a game?"

"No, not a game!" cried the captain. "We're from Earth."

"Out of the *ground*, do you mean?" she wondered.

"No, we came from the third planet, Earth, in a ship. And we've landed here on the fourth planet, Mars—"

"This," explained the woman, as if she were addressing a child, "is Green Bluff, Illinois, on the continent of America, surrounded by the Atlantic and Pacific oceans, on a place called the world, or, sometimes, the Earth. Go away now. Good-by."

She trotted down the hall, running her fingers through the beaded curtain.

The three men looked at one another.

"Let's knock the screen door in," said Lustig.

"We can't do that. This is private property. Good God!"

They went to sit down on the porch step.

"Did it ever strike you, Hinkston, that perhaps we got ourselves somehow, in some way, off track, and by accident came back and landed on Earth?"

"How could we have done that?"

"I don't know, I don't know. Oh God, let me think."

Hinkston said, "But we checked every mile of the way. Our chronometers said so many miles. We went past the Moon and out into space, and here we are. I'm *positive* we're on Mars."

Lustig said, "Suppose, by accident, in space, in time, we got lost in the dimensions and landed on an Earth that is thirty or forty years ago."

"Oh, go away, Lustig!"

Lustig went to the door, rang the bell, and called into the cool dim rooms: "What year is this?"

"Nineteen twenty-six, of course," said the lady, sitting in a rocking chair, taking a sip of her lemonade.

"Did you hear that?" Lustig turned wildly to the others. "Nineteen twenty-six! We *have* gone back in time! This *is* Earth!"

o o o

Lustig sat down, and the three men let the wonder and terror of the thought afflict them. Their hands stirred fitfully on their knees. The captain said, "I didn't ask for a thing like this. It scares the hell out of me. How can a thing like this happen? I wish we'd brought Einstein with us."

"Will anyone in this town believe us?" said Hinkston. "Are we playing with something dangerous? Time, I mean. Shouldn't we just take off and go home?"

They walked three houses down to a little white cottage under an oak tree. "I like to be as logical as I can be," said the captain. "And I don't believe we've put our finger on it yet. Suppose, Hinkston, as you originally suggested, that rocket travel occurred years ago? And when Earth people lived here a number of years they began to get homesick for Earth. First a mild neurosis about it, then a full-fledged psychosis. Then threatened insanity. What would you do as a psychiatrist if faced with such a problem?"

Hinkston thought. "Well, I think I'd rearrange the civilization on Mars so it resembled Earth more and more each day. If there was any way of reproducing every plant, every road, every lake . . . Then by some vast crowd hypnosis I'd convince everyone in a town this size that this really *was* Earth, not Mars at all."

"Good enough, Hinkston. I think we're on the right track now. That woman in that house back there just *thinks* she's living on Earth. It protects her sanity. She and all the others in this town are the patients of the greatest experiment in migration and hypnosis you will ever lay eyes on in your life."

"That's *it*, sir!" cried Lustig.

"Right!" said Hinkston.

"Well," the captain sighed. "Now we've got somewhere. I feel better. It's all a bit more logical. That talk about time and going back and forth and traveling through time turns my stomach upside down. But *this* way—" The captain smiled. "Well, well, it looks as if we'll be fairly popular here."

"Or will we?" said Lustig. "After all, like the Pilgrims, these people came here to escape Earth. Maybe they won't be too happy to see us. Maybe they'll try to drive us out or kill us."

"We have superior weapons. This next house now. Up we go."

But they had hardly crossed the lawn when Lustig stopped and looked off across the town, down the quiet, dreaming afternoon street. "Sir," he said.

"What is it, Lustig?"

"Oh, sir, *sir*, what *see*—" said Lustig, and he began to cry. His fingers came up, twisting and shaking, and his face was all wonder and joy and incredulity. He sounded as if at any moment he might go quite insane with happiness. He looked down the street and began to run, stumbling awkwardly, falling, picking himself up, and running on. "Look, look!"

"Don't let him get away!" the captain broke into a run.

Now Lustig was running swiftly, shouting. He turned into a yard halfway down the shady street and leaped up upon the porch of a large green house with an iron rooster on the roof.

He was beating at the door, hollering and crying, when Hinkston and the captain ran up behind him. They were all gasping and wheezing, exhausted from their run in the thin air. "Grandma! Grandpa!" cried Lustig.

Two old people stood in the doorway.

"David!" their voices piped, and they rushed out to embrace and pat him on the back and move around him. "David, it's been so many years! How you've grown, boy; how big you are, boy. Oh, David boy, how are you?"

"Grandma, Grandpa!" sobbed David Lustig. "You look fine, fine!" He held them, turned them, kissed them, hugged them, cried on them, held them out again, blinking at the little old people. The sun was in the sky, the wind blew, the grass was green, the screen door stood wide.

"Come in, boy, come in. There's iced tea for you, fresh, lots of it!"

"I've got friends here." Lustig turned and waved at the captain and Hinkston frantically, laughing.

"Captain, come on up."

"Howdy," said the old people. "Come in. Any friends of David's are our friends too. Don't stand there!"

o   o   o

In the living room of the old house it was cool, and a grandfather clock ticked high and long and bronzed in one corner. There were soft pillows on large couches and walls filled with books and a rug cut in a thick rose pattern, and iced tea in the hand, sweating, and cool on the thirsty tongue.

"Here's to our health," Grandma tipped her glass to her porcelain teeth.

"How long you been here, Grandma?" Lustig asked.

"Ever since we died," she said tartly.

"Ever since you what?" Captain John Black set down his glass.

"Oh yes." Lustig nodded. "They've been dead thirty years."

"And you sit there calmly!" shouted the captain.

"Tush." The old woman winked glitteringly. "Who are you to question what happens? Here we are. What's life, anyway? Who does what for why and where? All we know is here we are, alive again, and no questions asked. A second chance." She toddled over and held out her thin wrist. "Feel." The captain felt. "Solid, ain't it?" she asked. He nodded. "Well, then," she said triumphantly, "why go around questioning?"

"Well," said the captain, "it's simply that we never thought we'd find a thing like this on Mars."

"And now you've found it. I dare say there's lots on every planet that'll show you God's infinite ways."

"Is this heaven?" asked Hinkston.

"Nonsense, no. It's a world and we get a second chance. Nobody told us why. But then nobody told us why we were on Earth, either. That other Earth, I mean. The one you came from. How do we know there wasn't *another* before *that* one?"

"A good question," said the captain.

Lustig kept smiling at his grandparents. "Gosh, it's good to see you. Gosh, it's good."

The captain stood up and slapped his hand on his leg in a casual fashion. "We've got to be going. Thank you for the drinks."

"You'll be back, of course," said the old people. "For supper tonight?"

"We'll try to make it, thanks. There's so much to be done. My men are waiting for me back at the rocket and—"

He stopped. He looked toward the door, startled.

Far away in the sunlight there was a sound of voices, a shouting and a great hello.

"What's that?" asked Hinkston.

"We'll soon find out." And Captain John Black was out the front door abruptly, running across the green lawn into the street of the Martian town.

He stood looking at the rocket. The ports were open and his crew was streaming out, waving their hands. A crowd of people had gathered, and in and through and among these people the members of the crew were hurrying, talking, laughing, shaking hands. People did little dances. People swarmed. The rocket lay empty and abandoned.

A brass band exploded in the sunlight, flinging off a gay tune from upraised tubas and trumpets. There was a bang of drums and a shrill of fifes. Little girls with golden hair jumped up and down. Little boys shouted, "Hooray!" Fat men passed around ten-cent cigars. The town mayor made a speech. Then each member of the crew, with a mother on one arm, a father or sister on the other, was spirited off down the street into little cottages or big mansions.

"Stop!" cried Captain Black.

The doors slammed shut.

The heat rose in the clear spring sky, and all was silent. The brass band banged off around a corner, leaving the rocket to shine and dazzle alone in the sunlight.

"Abandoned!" said the captain. "They abandoned the ship, they did! I'll have their skins, by God! They had orders!"

"Sir," said Lustig, "don't be too hard on them. Those were all old relatives and friends."

"That's no excuse!"

"But how would you have felt, Captain?

"They had their orders, damn it!"

"But how would you have felt, Captain?"

"I would have obeyed orders—" The captain's mouth remained open.

Striding along the sidewalk under the Martian sun, tall, smiling, eyes amazingly clear and blue, came a young man of some twenty-six years. "John!" the man called out and broke into a trot.

"What?" Captain John Black swayed.

"John, you old son of a bitch!"

The man ran up and gripped his hand and slapped him on the back.

"It's you," said Captain Black.

"Of course, who'd you *think* it was?"

"Edward!" The captain appealed now to Lustig and Hinkston, holding the stranger's hand. "This is my brother Edward. Ed, meet my men, Lustig, Hinkston! My brother!"

They tugged at each other's hands and arms and then finally embraced. "Ed!"

"John, you bum, you!"

"Ed, Ed what *is* this?"

"Mom's waiting," said Edward Black, grinning.

"Mom?"

"And Dad, too."

"Dad?" The captain almost fell as if he had been hit by a mighty weapon. He walked stiffly and without coordination. "Mom and Dad alive? Where?"

"At the old house on Oak Knoll Avenue."

"The old house." The captain stared in delighted amaze. "Did you hear that, Lustig, Hinkston?"

Hinkston was gone. He had seen his own house down the street and was running for it. Lustig was laughing. "You see, Captain, what happened to everyone on the rocket? They couldn't help themselves."

"Yes. Yes." The captain shut his eyes. "When I open my eyes you'll be gone." He blinked. "You're still there. God, Ed, but you look *fine!*"

"Come on, lunch's waiting. I told Mom."

Lustig said, "Sir, I'll be with my grandfolks if you need me."

"What? Oh, fine, Lustig. Later, then."

Edward seized his arm and marched him. "There's the house. Remember it?"

"Hell! Bet I can beat you to the front porch!"

They ran. The trees roared over Captain Black's head; the earth roared under his feet. He saw the golden figure of Edward Black pull ahead of him in the amazing dream of reality. He saw the house rush forward, the screen door swing wide. "Beat you!" cried Edward. "I'm an old man," panted the captain, "and you're still young. But then, you *always* beat me, I remember!"

In the doorway, Mom, pink, plump, and bright. Behind her, pepper-gray, Dad, his pipe in his hand.

"Mom, Dad!"

He ran up the steps like a child to meet them.

o   o   o

It was a fine long afternoon. They finished a late lunch and they sat in the parlor and he told them all about his rocket and they nodded and smiled upon him and Mother was just the same and Dad bit the end off a cigar and lighted it thoughtfully in his old fashion. There was a big turkey dinner at night and time flowing on. When the drumsticks were sucked clean and lay brittle upon the plates, the captain leaned back and exhaled his deep satisfaction. Night was in all the trees and coloring the sky, and the lamps were halos of pink light in the gentle house. From all the other houses down the street came sounds of music, pianos playing, doors slamming.

Mom put a record on the victrola, and she and Captain John Black had a dance. She was wearing the same perfume he remembered from the summer when she and Dad had been killed in the train accident. She was very real in his arms as they danced lightly to the music. "It's not every day," she said, "you get a second chance to live."

"I'll wake in the morning," said the captain. "And I'll be in my rocket, in space, and all this will be gone."

"No, don't think that," she cried softly. "Don't question. God's good to us. Let's be happy."

"Sorry, Mom."

The record ended in a circular hissing.

"You're tired, Son." Dad pointed with his pipe. "Your old bedroom's waiting for you, brass bed and all."

"But I should report my men in."

"Why?"

"Why? Well, I don't know. No reason, I guess. No, none at all. They're all eating or in bed. A good night's sleep won't hurt them."

"Good night, Son." Mom kissed his cheek. "It's good to have you home."

"It's good to *be* home."

He left the land of cigar smoke and perfume and books and gentle light and ascended the stairs, talking, talking with Edward. Edward pushed a door open, and there was the yellow brass bed and the old semaphore banners from college and a very musty raccoon coat which he stroked with muted affection. "It's too much," said the captain. "I'm numb and I'm tired. I feel as if I'd been out in the pounding rain for forty-eight hours without an umbrella or a coat. I'm soaked to the skin with emotion."

Edward slapped wide the snowy linens and flounced the pillows. He slid the window up and let the night-blooming jasmine float in. There was moonlight and the sound of distant dancing and whispering.

"So this is Mars," said the captain, undressing.

"This is it." Edward undressed in idle, leisurely

moves, drawing his shirt off over his head, revealing golden shoulders and the good muscular neck.

The lights were out; they were in bed, side by side, as in the days how many decades ago? The captain lolled and was nourished by the scent of jasmine pushing the lace curtains out upon the dark air of the room. Among the trees, upon a lawn, someone had cranked up a portable phonograph and now it was playing softly. "Always."

The thought of Marilyn came to his mind.

"Is Marilyn here?

His brother, lying straight out in the moonlight from the window, waited and then said, "Yes. She's out of town. But she'll be here in the morning."

The captain shut his eyes. "I want to see Marilyn very much."

The room was square and quiet except for their breathing.

"Good night, Ed."

A pause. "Good night, John."

He lay peacefully, letting his thoughts float. For the first time the stress of the day was moved aside; he could think logically now. It had all been emotion. The bands playing, the familiar faces. But now . . .

How? he wondered. How was all this made? And why? For what purpose? Out of the goodness of some divine intervention? Was God, then, really that thoughtful of his children?

He considered the various theories advanced in the first heat of the afternoon by Hinkston and Lustig. He let all kinds of new theories drop in lazy pebbles down through his mind, turning, throwing out dull flashes of light. Mom. Dad. Edward. Mars. Earth. Mars. Martians.

Who had lived here a thousand years ago on Mars? Martians? Or had this always been the way it was today?

Martians. He repeated the word idly, inwardly.

He laughed out loud almost. He had the most ridiculous theory quite suddenly. It gave him a kind of chill. It was really nothing to consider, of course. Highly improbable. Silly. Forget it. Ridiculous.

But, he thought, just *suppose* . . . Just suppose, now, that there were Martians living on Mars and they saw our ship coming and saw us inside our ship and hated us. Suppose they wanted to destroy us, as invaders, as unwanted ones, and they wanted to do it in a very clever way, so that we would be taken off guard. Well, what would the best weapon be that a Martian could use against Earth Men with atomic weapons?

The answer was interesting. Telepathy, hypnosis, memory, and imagination.

Suppose all of these houses aren't real at all, this bed not real, but only figments of my own imagination, given substance by telepathy and hypnosis through the Martians, thought Captain John Black. Suppose these houses are really some *other* shape, a Martian shape, but, by playing on my desires and wants, these Martians have made this seem like my old home town, my old house, to lull me out of my suspicions. What better way to fool a man, using his own mother and father as bait?

And this town, so old, from the year 1926, long before *any* of my men were born. From a year when I was six years old and there *were* records of Harry Lauder, and Maxfield Parrish paintings *still* hanging, and bead curtains, and "Beautiful Ohio," and turn-of-the-century architecture. What if the Martians took the memories of a town *exclusively* from *my* mind? They say childhood memories are the clearest. And after they built the town from *my* mind, they populated it with the most-loved people from all the minds of the people on the rocket!

And suppose those two people in the next room, asleep, are not my mother and father at all. But two Martians, incredibly brilliant, with the ability to keep me under this dreaming hypnosis all of the time.

And that brass band today? What a startlingly wonderful plan it would be. First, fool Lustig, then Hinkston, then gather a crowd; and all the men in the rocket, seeing mothers, aunts, uncles, sweethearts, dead ten, twenty years ago, naturally, disregarding orders, rush out and abandon ship. What more natural? What more unsuspecting? What more simple? A man doesn't ask too many questions when his mother is suddenly brought back to life; he's much too happy. And here we all are tonight, in various houses, in various beds, with no weapons to protect us, and the rocket lies in the moonlight, empty. And wouldn't it be horrible and terrifying to discover that all of this was part of some great clever plan by the Martians to divide and conquer us, and kill us? Sometime during the night, perhaps, my brother here on this bed will change form, melt, shift, and become another thing, a terrible thing, a Martian. It would be very simple for him just to turn over in bed and put a knife into my heart. And in all those other houses down the street, a dozen other brothers or fathers suddenly melting away and taking knives and doing things to the unsuspecting, sleeping men of Earth. . . .

His hands were shaking under the covers. His body was cold. Suddenly it was not a theory. Suddenly he was very afraid.

He lifted himself in bed and listened. The night was very quiet. The music had stopped. The wind had died. His brother lay sleeping beside him.

Carefully he lifted the covers, rolled them back. He slipped from bed and was walking softly across the room when his brother's voice said, "Where are you going?"

"What?"

His brother's voice was quite cold. "I said, where do you think you're going?"

"For a drink of water."

"But you're not thirsty."

"Yes, yes, I am."

"No, you're not."

Captain John Black broke and ran across the room. He screamed. He screamed twice.

He never reached the door.

○ ○ ○

In the morning the brass band played a mournful dirge. From every house in the street came little solemn processions bearing long boxes, and along the sun-filled street, weeping, came the grandmas and mothers and sisters and brothers and uncles and fathers, walking to the churchyard, where there were new holes freshly dug and new tombstones installed. Sixteen holes in all, and sixteen tombstones.

The mayor made a little sad speech, his face sometimes looking like the mayor, sometimes looking like something else.

Mother and Father Black were there, with Brother Edward, and they cried, their faces melting now from a familiar face into something else.

Grandpa and Grandma Lustig were there, weeping, their faces shifting like wax, shimmering as all things shimmer on a hot day.

The coffins were lowered. Someone murmured about "the unexpected and sudden deaths of sixteen fine men during the night—"

Earth pounded down on the coffin lids.

The brass band, playing "Columbia, the Gem of the Ocean," marched and slammed back into town, and everyone took the day off.

(By Mr. Bradbury's request, this story appears in its entirety here and is not the abridged version that appeared in Read *magazine.)*

OBEDIENCE

BY FREDRIC BROWN

o   o   o

**In his world, obedience ruled.
Death was the punishment for
those who dared to disobey.**

On a tiny planet of a far, faint star, invisible from Earth and at the farther edge of the galaxy is a statue of an Earth human. Made of precious metal, it is a tremendous thing, fully 10 inches high, exquisite in workmanship.

Bugs crawl on it . . .

o   o   o

They were on a routine patrol in Sector 1534, out past the Dog Star. The ship was the usual two-man scout used for all patrols outside the solar system. Captain May and Lieutenant Ross were playing chess when the alarm rang.

Captain May said, "Reset it, Don, while I think this out." He didn't look up from the board; he knew the thing out there had to be a passing meteor. In this sector there was nothing else it could be.

Ross didn't get up either, but he turned around in his chair to face the instrument board and the telescreen. He glanced up casually and gasped; there *was* a ship on the screen. He got his breath back enough to say, "Cap!" and then the chessboard was on the floor and May was looking over his shoulder.

He could hear the sound of May's breathing, and then May's voice said, "Fire, Don!"

"But that's a Rochester Class cruiser! One of ours. I don't know what it's doing here, but we can't—"

"*Look again.*"

Suddenly Don Ross saw what May had meant. It was almost a Rochester, but not quite. There was something *alien* about it. Something? It *was* alien; it was an alien imitation of a Rochester. Ross's hands raced for the firing button almost before the full impact of that hit him.

Finger at the button, he looked at the dials on the Picar ranger finder and the Monold detector. They stood at zero.

Ross swore. "He's jamming us, Cap. We can't figure out how far he is or his size and mass!"

Captain May nodded slowly, his face pale.

Inside Don Ross's head, a thought said, "*Compose yourselves, humans. We are not enemies.*"

Ross turned and stared at May. May said, "Yes, I got it. Telepathy."

Ross swore again. *If they were telepathic—*

"Fire. Visual."

Ross pressed the button, and the screen filled with a flare of energy. When the energy subsided, there was no wreckage of a spaceship . . .

0   0   0

Admiral Sutherland turned his back to the star chart on the wall and regarded the two men sourly. He said, "I am not interested in rehashing your formal report, Captain May. You are here for discipline, and you know the penalty for disobedience."

May said stiffly, "Yes, sir."

"It is?"

"Death, sir."

"And what order did you disobey?"

"General order Thirteen-Ninety, Section Twelve, Quad-A priority: Any Earth ship, military or otherwise, will destroy immediately any alien ship encountered. If it fails to do so, the Earth ship must blast off toward outer space and continue until fuel is exhausted."

"And the reason for that, Captain?"

"So there is no possibility, Sir, of the alien ship following the sighting ship back to Earth."

"Yet you disobeyed that ruling, Captain. You were not certain that you had destroyed the alien, but you failed to head for outer space. Why?"

"We did not think it necessary, sir. The aliens did not seem hostile. Besides, sir, they must already know our base; they addressed us as 'humans.'"

"Nonsense! The telepathic message was broadcast from an alien mind, but was received by yours. Your minds automatically translated the message into your own words. The aliens did not necessarily know your point of origin or that you were humans."

Lieutenant Ross had no business speaking, but he did. "Then, sir, it is not believed that the aliens were friendly?"

The admiral snorted. "Where did you take your training, Lieutenant? You seemed to have missed the most basic premise of our defense plans: *Any alien is an enemy*. Even though he is friendly today, how can we know that he will be friendly next year or a century from now?"

Admiral Sutherland leaned forward and continued, "Look at the military history of the world! It proves that, if it proves nothing else. Look at Rome! To be safe, she couldn't afford powerful neighbors. Alexander the Great! Napoleon! They had the same policy."

"Sir," asked Captain May, "am I under the penalty of death?"

"Yes."

"Then I may as well speak. Where is Rome now? Where is Alexander's empire or Napoleon's? Nazi Germany? Where is *Tyrannosaurus rex*?"

Admiral Sutherland looked puzzled by the last name.

"Who?"

"*Tyrannosaurus rex*, the fiercest of the dinosaurs. His name means 'king of the tyrant lizards.' He thought every other creature was his enemy too. Where is he now? Extinct."

"Is that all you have to say, Captain?" the admiral spoke coldly.

"Yes, Sir."

"Then I shall overlook it. Mistaken, sentimental reasoning. You are *not* under sentence of death, Captain. I merely said so to see how far you would go. However, you are not being shown mercy because of any humanitarian nonsense. A special circumstance has changed matters."

"May I ask what, sir?"

"The alien *was* destroyed. Your Picar and Monold were working properly. The only reason that they did not register was that the alien ship was too small. The instrument will register a meteor weighing as little as 5 pounds. The alien ship was smaller than that."

"Smaller than——?"

"You were thinking of alien life in terms of your own size. There is no reason why it should be. It could be even microscopic, too small to be visible. The alien ship must have contacted you at a distance of only a few feet. Your fire, at that distance, destroyed it utterly. That is why you saw no charred hulk as evidence that it was destroyed."

He smiled. "My congratulations, gentlemen."

Ross said, "Don't you think that the fact that the ship we saw, regardless of size, was an imitation of one of our Rochester Class ships is proof that the aliens already knew much more of us than we do of them? That would include the location of our home planet."

The admiral frowned. "Perhaps. Obviously they are quite inferior to us technically or *they* would not imitate our design in spaceships. They must have read the minds of our engineers in order to copy that design. At any rate, it is up to us to find and exterminate them before they find us. Even microscopic aliens are a threat to our civilization. You reminded me of history, Captain May. Now I shall remind you of another chapter from history—the Plague." The admiral sat at his desk. "Every Earth ship in space is on alert for these aliens. A state of war exists. A state of war always exists with aliens. That is all, gentlemen. You may go."

Outside in the corridor two armed guards waited. One of them stepped to each side of Captain May. May said quickly, "Don't say anything, Don. I expected this. I disobeyed an important order. Keep yourself out of it."

Hands clenched, teeth clamped together, Don Ross watched the guards take away his friend. He knew May was right. Ross could do nothing except get himself into trouble or make things worse for May.

Ross walked almost blindly out of the Admiralty Building. He had the usual two-weeks' leave before reporting back for space duty. He knew he'd better straighten himself out mentally in that time. He reported to a psychiatrist and let himself be talked out of most of his bitterness and feeling of rebellion.

He watched the telenewscasts avidly during that period and learned that in various other sectors of space, four more alien ships had been found. All were destroyed on sight. There had been no communication after first contact.

On the tenth day of his leave, Ross ended it of his own free will. He returned to the Admiralty Building and asked for an audience with Admiral Sutherland. He was laughed at, of course, but he had expected that. He managed to get a brief verbal message carried through to the admiral. Simply: "I know a plan that may let us find the planet of the aliens, at no risk to ourselves."

That got him in, all right.

He stood at rigid attention before the admiral's desk. He said, "Sir, the aliens have been trying to contact us. We have destroyed them on contact before a complete telepathic thought has been communicated. If we permit them to communicate, there is a chance that they will give away, accidentally or otherwise, the location of their home planet."

Admiral Sutherland said dryly, "And whether they do or not, they might find out *ours* by following the ship back."

"Sir, my plan covers that. I suggest that I be sent out into the same sector where first contact was made—this time in a one-man ship, *unarmed*. The fact that I am doing so should be publicized as widely as possible so that every man in space knows it—and knows too that I am in an unarmed ship for the purpose of making contact with the aliens."

Admiral Sutherland looked interested. "Go on."

"If news of my mission is known to the entire fleet, it will reach the aliens. Knowing that my ship is unarmed, they will make contact. Possibly the message will include a clue to the location of their home planet."

Admiral Sutherland said, "And in that case their planet would last all of 24 hours. But what about the possibility of their following you back?"

"That, Sir, is where we have nothing to lose. I shall return to Earth *only if I find out that they already know its location.*"

Admiral Sutherland stared at Ross. He said, "Son, you *have* got something. It may cost your life; but, if it doesn't and if you come back with news of where the aliens come from, you're going to be the hero of the race. You'll probably end up with *my* job. In fact, I'm tempted to steal your idea and make the trip myself."

"Sir, you're too valuable. I'm expendable."

The admiral cleared his throat and was silent for a moment. Then he said, "Go to it, Lieutenant. Rather, go to it, *Captain.*"

"Thank you, sir."

"A ship will be ready for you in three days. We could have it ready sooner, but it will take that long for word of your mission to spread throughout the fleet. You understand, you are not under any circumstances to deviate from the plan that you have outlined."

"Yes, Sir. Obedience. I understand. Unless the aliens already know the location of Earth and prove it completely, I shall not return. I shall blast off into space. I give you my word, sir."

"Very good, Captain Ross."

o   o   o

The one-man spacer hovered near the center of Sector 1534, out past the Dog Star. No other ship patrolled that sector. Captain Don Ross sat quietly and waited. He watched the visiplate and listened for a voice to speak inside his head.

It came when he had waited less than three hours. *Greetings, Donross*, the voice said, and simultaneously there were five tiny spaceships outside his visiplate. His Monold showed that they weighed less than an ounce apiece.

He said, "Shall I talk aloud or merely think?"

It does not matter. You may speak if you wish to

concentrate on a particular thought, but first be silent for a moment.

After half a minute, Ross thought he heard the echo of a sigh in his mind. Then: *I am sorry. I fear this talk will do neither of us any good. You see, Donross, we do not know the location of your home planet. We could have learned, perhaps, but we were not interested. We are not hostile, and from the minds of Earth humans, we knew we dared not be friendly. If you obey orders, you will never return to Earth to make your report.*

Don Ross closed his eyes a moment. This, then, was the end. He had given his word to Admiral Sutherland that he would obey orders to the letter.

That is right, said the voice. *We are both doomed, Donross, and it does not matter now what we tell you. We cannot get through the cordon of your ships, we have lost half our race trying.*

"Half! Do you mean—?"

Yes. There were only a thousand of us left at the time we abandoned our planet. Of ten ships, five have been destroyed by Earthlings. Those you see now are all that is left of our civilization. Our entire race. Would it interest you, even though you are going to die, to know about us?

Ross nodded, forgetting that they could not see him, but the yes in his mind must have been read.

We are an old race, much older than you. Our home is—or was—a tiny planet of the dark companion of Sirius. Your ships have not found it yet, but they will in time. We have been intelligent for millions of years, but we never developed space travel. There was no need and we had no desire.

Twenty of your years ago, an Earth ship passed near our planet, and we caught the thoughts of the men upon it. We knew your human quest to conquer space. We knew from those human thoughts that we would be found sooner or later, if we stayed on our planet. We also knew that we would be ruthlessly exterminated upon discovery. Our only chance of survival lay in immediate flight to the farthest limits of the galaxy.

"You did not think of fighting back?"

No. We could not have, had we wished—and we did not wish. It is impossible for us to kill. If the death of one single human, even of a lesser creature, would ensure our survival, we could not bring about that death. That you cannot understand. Wait—I see that you can understand. You are not like other Earthlings, Donross.

"There are others like me, though perhaps not enough." He shook his head. "Tell me the rest of your story."

We took details of space travel from the minds of members of the Earth ships that entered our space. We adapted them to the tiny scale of the ships we built. We failed in our effort to escape. We underestimated the net with which your race has cordoned space. We cannot escape through your patrols.

Don Ross said grimly, "I destroyed one of your ships. Did you know that?"

You merely obeyed orders. Do not blame yourself. Obedience is almost as deeply rooted in your species as hatred of killing is in us. When we learned that you were attempting to contact us with an unarmed ship, we decided that perhaps one last contact was worth the risk. In reading your thoughts, however, I realize that our initial understanding of your race was accurate. Even if you disobeyed orders and returned to Earth to report what we have just told you, no orders would be issued to let us through. Possibly in future ages, by the time humans reach the far edge of the galaxy, there will be more like you. For now, the chances of our getting even one of our five ships through is remote.

Good-bye, Donross. But what is this strange emotion in your mind and the convulsion of your muscles? I do not understand.

Don Ross managed finally to stop laughing. "Listen, my alien friend who cannot kill," he said, "I'm getting you out of this. I'm going to see that you get through our cordon to the safety you want. What's funny is the way I'm going to do it. By obedience to orders. I'm going to outer space."

You will die.

"And you will live. Hitchhike. Your tiny ships won't show on the patrol's detectors if they are touching this ship. We will be far beyond the reach of any detectors when my fuel runs out."

Inside Don Ross's head was only silence. And then, faintly, softly came this thought: *Thank you.*

He waited until the five ships had vanished from his visiplate and he had heard five tiny sounds of their touching the hull of his own ship. He laughed once more. Then, obeying orders, Don Ross blasted off for deep space and death.

0   0   0

On a tiny planet of a far, faint star, invisible from Earth, and at the farther edge of the galaxy, five times as far as man has yet penetrated into space, is the statue of an Earth human. Made of precious metal, it is a tremendous thing, fully 10 inches high, exquisite in workmanship.

Bugs crawl on it, but they have a right to. They made it, and they honor it. The statue is of very hard metal. On an airless world it will last forever—or until Earthlings find it and blast it out of existence. Unless, of course, by that time Earthlings have changed an awful lot.

PART 3

WHAT WILL BE THE FUTURE

o o o

In the twenty-first century and beyond,
the future will exist in the minds—and
memories—of the dreamers.

GOOD MORNING! THIS IS THE FUTURE

TWO SHORT-SHORTS BY HENRY SLESAR

o   o   o

**The two men had it all figured out.
Go to sleep now and wake up in the future
to claim your reward. But . . .**

A.D. 2496

He awoke in warm fluid, to wordless sounds of comfort. Then he was being lifted from the rotobath by mechanical hands that were as gentle as a woman's. He was like an infant reborn and just as naked. His weight at birth was 206 pounds, most of it flab.

After a while, they let him sit up. He asked for a cigar, and the request provoked confusion and some laughter. One of the white-coated attendants whispered an explanation to his younger assistant. The young man looked ill at the description of *cigar*.

Then the questions.

"Your name is Jervis T. Murath?"

"Yes."

"Your age upon entering suspension?"

"Fifty-one."

"You were a member of the financial community prior to entering the Dormantory?"

"Was," Murath growled. "Wiped out in the crash of '97. Scrounged up just enough money to make this trip. And a little extra," he added craftily.

"Your orientation classes will begin tomorrow," the attendant said. "Attendance is voluntary."

"Don't want any classes. Just want to know one thing. Is there still a First Central Bank of Chicago?"

"I will call Information."

The attendant spoke to a glowing patch in the wall and then returned.

"The First Central Bank of Chicago is now one of a group of consolidated banking institutions known as the Midwestern Trust Company. All accounts have been preserved intact. You may make deposits or withdrawals at any one of MTC's 6,400 branch offices."

"Where is the nearest one?" Murath asked.

The bank building was the shape and color of an egg; the money was of many colors and quite pretty. Murath was seated in front of a transparent bubble that encased a teller.

"My name is Jervis T. Murath," he said. "I opened an account at the First Central in 1985 with two thousand dollars. The interest rate was 7 percent, compounded semiannually. I don't imagine it stayed the same."

"No, sir," the teller said. "The interest rate has varied from between nothing at all to 22 percent in the last 500 years. One moment, please, while I check your record."

Murath held his breath and wished he had a cigar.

The teller reappeared.

"Your money is on deposit," he said. "The total is 54 million, 700 thousand, 854 dollars, and 4 cents."

"Thank you," Murath said joyfully. "I'd like 50 thousand in cash right now."

He left the bank with the money in his pocket. Across the street was an immense circular building with moving ramps. From the crowds and the packages, he gathered that it was a department store.

He walked into the store and chuckled with pleasure at the sight of the marvelous merchandise. An attractive young woman in a short blue uniform came to his side.

"I'm your Shopper," she said. "May I help you?"

"You sure can," he grinned. "I need just about everything." He looked at his out-of-date costume. "Clothes first. How much is that shirt over there?"

"Handsome, isn't it?" the young woman smiled. "And it's on sale too. Only 400 thousand dollars."

◊   ◊   ◊

A.D. 2911

Lamb was no longer in the Dormantory. He was in a strangely dimensionless room whose walls seemed to be composed of light. The temperature was cooler than he liked, and he was without clothing or blankets. On the airy strip of foam, his thin body shivered.

"Chilly in here," he told the hairless man standing next to him.

"The temp's at the ideal constant," he was told. "You'll get used to it. Your name is James Percy Lamb?"

"That's right. Are you a doctor?"

"No, Mr. Lamb." He laughed. "Not the sort you mean. You'll find that the medical profession no longer exists in the form you knew. There is the Accident Division and the Prevention Corps, of course. But from your Dormantory application, it's obvious that you expect a pathologist."

"Then you know," Lamb said nervously, licking his lips. "Can you help me? Have you found the cure?"

"Be at peace, my friend. Your illness is a thing of the past. Generations ago, we totally wiped out all disease."

"Then I was right," Lamb whispered. "I knew I was doing the right thing. I would have died in my own time . . ."

"You'll be fine for now. We are preparing the cure for your specific ailment. It will take a few hours, since there has been no need of it for many years. Just be comfortable and wait."

He was left alone, shivering.

Eventually, from the doorway of light, two more hairless men entered. One of them carried a roundheaded syringe.

"Here we are," he said jovially. "The pressure syringe will put the antidote into your bloodstream in five seconds. We expect the antibodies will form within the next eight or nine hours."

The head of the syringe was placed against his bare, goosefleshed arm. He felt nothing, but he was asleep by the time they left. In what may have been the morning, he woke again, and found his body being explored with a glowing cylinder that seemed to penetrate his flesh.

"What is this?" he asked

"Diagnosis," the hairless man said. "We are quite satisfied, Mr. Lamb. The disease is completely erased from your system." He flicked off the cylinder's glow.

Lamb began to cry. "Thank God," he said, sniffling, his eyes running.

Then he sneezed.

"What was that?" the hairless man said, springing backward.

"Nothing, just a sneeze. I got a little chill last night. I guess I caught a cold."

"A cold? A *cold!*" the man said in horror.

He dashed from the room, and returned quickly with two others. Their smooth faces were anxious.

"What's the matter?" Lamb said and sneezed again. "I told you, it's only a cold."

"Better call the Prevention Corps," one of them muttered.

The uniformed officers entered half an hour later. They wore hoods over their heads, and approached him warily. They pinned his arms, and gave him a swift, painless injection that ended his life, and the threat of infection, in five minutes.

HARRISON BERGERON

BY KURT VONNEGUT JR.

◊   ◊   ◊

**In Harrison's world, everyone is
perfectly average. And the Handicapper
General intends to keep it that way.**

The year was 2081, and everybody was finally
equal. They weren't only equal before God and the
law, they were equal every which way. Nobody was
smarter than anybody else; nobody was better looking than anybody else; nobody was stronger or
quicker than anybody else. All this equality was
due to the 211th, 212th, and 213th Amendments
of the Constitution—and to the unceasing vigi-
lance of agents of the United States Handicapper
General.

Some things about living still weren't quite
right, though. April, for instance, still drove people
crazy by not being springtime. And it was in that
clammy month that the H-G men took George and

Hazel Bergeron's fourteen-year-old son, Harrison, away.

It was tragic, all right, but George and Hazel had a perfectly average intelligence, which meant she couldn't think about anything except in short bursts. And George, while his intelligence was way above normal, had a little mental handicap radio in his ear. He was required by law to wear it at all times. It was tuned to a government transmitter, and every twenty seconds or so, the transmitter would send out some sharp noise to keep people like George from taking unfair advantage of their brains.

George and Hazel were watching television. There were tears on Hazel's cheeks, but she'd forgotten for the moment what they were about.

On the television screen, ballerinas came to the end of a dance, and a buzzer sounded in George's head. His thoughts fled in panic, like bandits from a burglar alarm.

"That was a real pretty dance, that dance they just did," said Hazel.

"Huh?" said George.

"That dance on TV—it was nice."

"Yup," said George. He tried to think a little about the ballerinas. They weren't really very good—

no better than anyone else would have been, anyway. They were burdened with sash weights and bags of birdshot, and their faces were masked. No one could see a free and graceful gesture or a pretty face, and by comparison feel like something the cat dragged in. George was toying with the notion that maybe dancers shouldn't be handicapped. Before he got very far with that idea, another noise in his ear radio scattered his thoughts.

George winced. So did two out of the eight ballerinas.

0   0   0

Hazel saw him wince. Having no mental handicap herself, she had to ask George what the latest sound had been.

"Sounded like somebody hitting a milk bottle with a sledgehammer."

"I'd think it would be real interesting, hearing all the different sounds," said Hazel, a little envious. "The things they think up."

"Um," said George.

"Only, if I was Handicapper General, you know what I would do?" said Hazel.

As a matter of fact, Hazel bore a strong resemblance to the Handicapper General, a woman named Diana Moon Glampers. "If I was Diana Moon Glampers," said Hazel, "I'd have chimes on Sunday—just chimes. Kind of in honor of religion."

"I could think, if it was just chimes," said George.

"Well—maybe make 'em real loud," said Hazel. "I think I'd make a good Handicapper General."

"Good as anybody else," said George.

"Who knows better'n I do what normal is?" said Hazel.

"Right," said George. He began to think glimmeringly about his abnormal son who was now in jail, about Harrison. But just then a twenty-one-gun salute in his head stopped that.

"Boy!" said Hazel, "that was a doozy, wasn't it?"

It was such a doozy that George was white and trembling, and tears stood on the rims of his red eyes. On the television screen, two of the eight ballerinas had collapsed to the studio floor, holding their temples.

"All of a sudden you look so tired," said Hazel. "Why don't you stretch out on the sofa so's you can rest your handicap bag on the pillows, honeybunch?" She was referring to the forty-seven-pound bag of bird shot padlocked around George's neck.

"Go on and rest the bag for a little while," Hazel said. "I don't care if you're not equal to me for a while."

George weighed the bag with his hands. "I don't mind it anymore," he said. "It's just a part of me."

"You been so tired lately—kind of wore out," said Hazel. "If there was just some way we could make a little hole in the bottom of the bag, and just take out a few of them lead weights."

"Two years in prison and $2,000 fine for every weight I took out," said George. "It wouldn't be worth it."

"If you could just take a few out when you came home from work," said Hazel. "I mean—you don't compete with anybody around here. You just set around."

"If I tried to get away with it," said George, "then other people'd get away with it—and pretty soon we'd be back to the dark ages again, with everybody competing against everybody else. You wouldn't like that, would you?"

"I'd hate it," said Hazel.

"There you are," said George. "The minute people start cheating on laws, what do you think happens to society?"

If Hazel hadn't been able to come up with an answer to this question, George couldn't have supplied one. A siren was going off in his head.

"Reckon it'd fall all apart," said Hazel.

"What would?" said George blankly.

"Society," said Hazel uncertainly. "Wasn't that what you just said?"

"Who knows?" said George.

o   o   o

The television program was suddenly interrupted for a news bulletin. It wasn't clear at first what the bulletin was about, since the announcer, like all announcers, had a serious speech impediment. For about half a minute, and in a state of high excitement, the announcer tried to say, "Ladies and gentlemen—"

He finally gave up and handed the bulletin to a ballerina to read.

"That's all right," Hazel said of the announcer. "He tried. That's the big thing. He tried to do the best he could with what God gave him. He should get a nice raise for trying so hard."

"Ladies and gentlemen—" said the ballerina, reading the bulletin. She must have been extraordinarily beautiful because the mask she wore was hideous. And it was easy to see that she was the strongest and most graceful of the dancers, for her handicap sacks were as big as those worn by two-hundred-pound men.

And she had to apologize at once for her voice, which was like a luminous timeless melody. It was a very unfair voice for a woman to use.

"Excuse me—" she said and began again, this time making her voice absolutely uncompetitive.

"Harrison Bergeron, age fourteen," she said in grackle squawk, "has just escaped from jail, where he was held on suspicion of plotting to overthrow the government. He is a genius and an athlete. He is underhandicapped and is extremely dangerous."

A police photograph of Harrison Bergeron was flashed on the screen—upside down, then sideways, upside down again, then right-side up. The picture showed the full length of Harrison against a background calibrated in feet and inches. He was exactly seven feet tall.

The rest of Harrison's appearance was Halloween and hardware. Nobody had ever borne heavier handicaps. He had outgrown hindrances faster than the H-G men could think them up. Instead of a little ear radio for a mental handicap, he wore a tremendous pair of earphones, and spectacles with thick, wavy lenses. The spectacles were intended to make him half blind and give him whanging head-aches.

Scrap metal was hung all over him. Ordinarily, there was a certain symmetry, a military neatness to the handicaps issued to strong people. But Harrison looked like a walking junkyard. In the race of life, Harrison carried three hundred pounds.

And to offset his good looks, the H-G men required that he wear at all times a red rubber ball for a nose, keep his eyebrows shaved off, and cover his even teeth with black caps at snaggletooth random.

"If you see this boy," said the ballerina, "do not—I repeat, do not—try to reason with him."

She was interrupted by a shriek and the sound of a door being torn from its hinges.

Screams and barking cries of distress came from the television set. The photograph of Harrison Bergeron on the screen jumped again and again, as though dancing to an earthquake.

George Bergeron correctly identified the earth-quake, and well he might have. Many was the time his own home had danced to the same crashing tune.

"That must be Harrison!" said George. "That's our son."

o   o   o

The realization was blasted from his mind instantly by the sound of an automobile collision in his head.

When George could open his eyes again, the photograph of Harrison was gone. A living, breathing Harrison filled the screen.

Clanking, clownish, and huge, Harrison stood in the center of the studio. The knob of the uprooted studio door was still in his hand. Ballerinas, technicians, musicians, and announcers cowered on their knees before him, expecting to die.

"I am the Emperor!" cried Harrison. "Do you hear? I am the Emperor! Everybody must do what I say at once!" He stamped his foot and the studio shook.

"Even as I stand here," he bellowed, "crippled, hobbled, sickened—I am a greater ruler than any man who ever lived! Now watch me become what I *can* become!"

Harrison tore the straps of his handicap harness as if they were wet tissue paper—straps guaranteed to support five thousand pounds.

The handicaps of metal and scrap iron crashed to the floor.

Harrison thrust his thumbs under the bar of the padlock that secured his head harness. The bar snapped like celery.

Harrison smashed his headphones and spectacles against the wall.

He flung away his rubber-ball nose, revealing a man that would have awed Thor, the god of thunder.

"I shall now select my Empress!" he said, looking down on the cowering people. "Let the first woman who dares rise to her feet and share my throne!"

A moment passed, and then a ballerina arose, swaying like a willow.

Harrison plucked the mental handicap from her ear and snapped off her physical handicaps with marvelous delicacy. Last of all, he removed her mask.

She was blindingly beautiful.

"Now—" said Harrison, taking her hand. "Shall we show the people the meaning if the word *dance*? Music!" he commanded.

The musicians scrambled back into their chairs, and Harrison stripped them of their handicaps, too. "Play your best," he told them, "and I'll make you barons and dukes and earls."

The music began. It was normal at first— cheap, silly, false. But Harrison snatched two musicians from their chairs, waved them like batons, and sang the music as he wanted it played. He slammed them back into their chairs.

The music began again and was much improved.

Harrison and his Empress merely listened to the music for a while—listened gravely, as though synchronizing their heartbeats with it.

Harrison placed his big hands on the girl's tiny waist, letting her sense the weightlessness that would soon be hers.

And then, in an explosion of joy and grace, into the air they sprang!

Not only were the laws of the land abandoned, but the law of gravity and the laws of motion as well.

They reeled, whirled, swiveled, capered, gamboled and spun. They leaped like deer on the moon.

The studio ceiling was thirty feet high, but each step brought the dancers nearer to it.

It became their obvious intention to kiss the ceiling.

They kissed it.

And then, overcoming gravity with love and pure will, they remained suspended in air, inches below the ceiling. And they kissed each other.

It was then that Diana Moon Glampers, the

Handicapper General, came into the studio with a double-barreled ten-gauge shotgun. She fired twice, and the Emperor and Empress were dead before they hit the floor.

Diana Moon Glampers loaded the gun again. She aimed it at the musicians and told them that they had ten seconds to get their handicaps back on.

It was then that Bergerons' television tube burned out.

o   o   o

Hazel turned to comment about the blackout to George. But George had gone out into the kitchen. When he returned, he paused a moment while a handicap signal shook him up. Then he sat down again. "You been crying?" he said to Hazel, watching her wipe tears away.

"Yup," she said.

"What about?" he said

"It's all kind of mixed up in my mind," said Hazel.

"Forget sad things," said George.

"I always do," said Hazel.

"That's my girl," said George. He winced. There was the sound of a riveting gun in his head.

"Gee—I could tell that one was a doozy," said Hazel.

"You can say that again," said George.

"Gee—" said Hazel—"I could tell that one was a doozy."

THE GIVER

THREE PASSAGES FROM THE AWARD-WINNING NOVEL
BY LOIS LOWRY

o o o

In The Giver's world, Sameness rules. Genetic experi-
mentation has done away with all ethnic cultures.
Everyone's skin color is the same. Careful control of
birth rates, career choices, and assignments of mates
ensures that no one is rich or poor. Even children are
alike. At 7 years of age, all girls wear ribbons in their
hair. At 9, all children get bikes. That way, no one is
made to feel inferior to anyone else.

    This perfect world has one other aspect absolutely
necessary to complete Sameness in people—lack of
memory. Only one person—The Giver—remembers
how the world used to be before Sameness. In his mind,
he holds all the memories in the world. But The Giver

*is an old man now, and 12-year-old Jonas has been
selected to take his place. During Jonas's training, The
Giver must transmit all his memories—both good and
bad—to the boy's mind.*

o   o   o

The Memory of Snow

Jonas felt nothing unusual at first. Then he shivered. At the same instant, breathing in, he felt the
air change, and his very breath was cold. He licked
his lips, and in doing so, his tongue touched the
suddenly chilled air.

Now he became aware of an entirely new sensation. Pinpricks? No, because they were soft and
without pain. Tiny, cold, featherlike feelings pep-
pered his body and face. He put out his tongue again
and caught one of the dots of cold upon it. The
sensation made him smile.

He could see a bright, whirling torrent of crys-
tals in the air around him, and he could see them
gather on the backs of his hands, like cold fur.

He was up high someplace. The ground was
thick with the furry snow, but he sat slightly above
it on a hard, flat object. *Sled,* he knew abruptly.
And the sled itself seemed to be poised at the top of

a long, extended mound that rose from the very land where he was.

Then the sled, with Jonas himself upon it, began to move through the snowfall, and he understood instantly that now he was going downhill. His face cut through the frigid air as he began the descent. Breathless glee overwhelmed him: the speed; the clear, cold air; the total silence; the feeling of balance and excitement and peace.

He opened his eyes. The old man was watching him. "Whew," said The Giver. "That was exhausting. But even transmitting that tiny memory to you lightened me just a little."

"Do you mean that you don't have the memory of it—of that ride on the sled—anymore?"

"That's right. A little weight off this old body."

"But it was such fun! And now you don't have it anymore! I *took* it!"

The old man laughed. "I have a whole world of memories to give you."

"Why don't we have snow and sleds and hills?" Jonas asked. "Did my parents have sleds when they were young? Did you?"

"No. It's a very distant memory. That's why it was so exhausting—I had to tug it forward from many generations back."

"But what happened to those things? Snow and the rest of it?"

"Climate control. Snow made growing food difficult. Unpredictable weather made transportation impossible at times. Snow wasn't practical, so it became obsolete when we went to Sameness."

Jonas frowned. "I wish we had those things, still."

The old man smiled. "So do I, but that choice is not ours."

o　o　o

The Memory of Color

Days went by, and weeks. Jonas learned, through the memories, the names of colors, and now he began to see them all in his ordinary life. But they didn't last. There would be a glimpse of green—the landscaped lawn around the Central Plaza; a bush on the riverbank. The bright orange of pumpkins being trucked in from the agricultural fields beyond the community boundary—seen in an instant, the flashing memory of brilliant color, then gone again, returning to their flat and hueless shade.

"I want them!" Jonas said angrily one day. "It isn't fair that nothing has color."

"Not fair?" The Giver looked at Jonas. "Explain what you mean."

"Well . . . " Jonas began, "if everything's the same, then there aren't any choices! I want to wake up in the morning and *decide* things! A blue tunic or a red one?" He looked down at the colorless fabric of his clothing. "But it's all the same, always."

"Our people made that choice, the choice to go to Sameness. Before my time, before the previous time, back and back. We gave up color when we gave up sunshine and did away with differences." He thought for a moment. "We gained control of many things. But we had to let go of others."

"We shouldn't have!" Jonas said fiercely. "I know it's not important what you wear. It doesn't matter if the tunic is blue or red, it's just—"

"It's just the choosing that's important, is that what you mean?"

Jonas nodded.

"But what if people made the wrong choices—not about color, about other things?"

"You mean like if they got to choose their own jobs or mates?"

"Frightening, isn't it?" The Giver said.

"So it's up to us to protect people from making the wrong choices?"

"It's safer that way."

"Yes," Jonas agreed. But for a long time afterward, Jonas felt a frustration that he didn't understand.

o o o

The Memory of War

One morning when Jonas arrived in the Annex Room, The Giver looked up at him, his face contorted with suffering. "Please," he gasped, "take some of the pain."

Jonas helped him to his chair. Then Jonas braced himself and entered the memory that was torturing The Giver.

He was in a confused, noisy, foul-smelling place. It was early morning, and the air was thick with smoke that hung, yellow and brown, above the ground. Around him lay groaning men. A wild-eyed horse, its bridle torn and dangling, trotted frantically, tossing its head, whinnying in panic. It stumbled, finally, then fell.

Jonas heard a voice next to him. "Water," the voice said in a parched, croaking whisper.

He turned his head toward the voice and looked into the half-closed eyes of a boy who seemed not much older than himself. Dirt streaked the boy's face and his matted blond hair. He lay sprawled, his gray uniform glistening with wet, fresh blood.

The boy stared at him. "Water," he begged again.

The noise continued all around: the cries of wounded men begging for water and for mother and for death. Horses lying on the ground shrieked, raised their heads, and stabbed randomly toward the sky with their hooves.

Jonas could hear the thud of cannons. Overwhelmed by pain, he lay there for hours, listened to the men and animals die, and learned what warfare meant. When he could bear it no longer, he opened his eyes and was in the Annex Room again.

The Giver looked away, as if he couldn't bear to see what he had done to Jonas. "Forgive me," he said.

"Why?" Jonas asked. "Why do you and I have to hold these memories?"

"It gives us wisdom," The Giver replied. "Without wisdom I could not fulfill my function of advising the Committee of Elders when they call upon me to make a choice for them."

"But why can't *everyone* have the memories? It would be easier if the memories were shared. Then you and I wouldn't have to bear so much by ourselves if everyone took a part."

The Giver sighed. "You're right," he said. "But then everyone would be burdened and pained. They don't want that. And that's the real reason. They selected me—and you—to lift that burden from themselves."

BY THE WATERS OF BABYLON

BY STEPHEN VINCENT BENÉT

o o o

**The journey was forbidden.
When the gods saw him, would he die?**

The north and the west and the south are good hunting ground, but it is forbidden to go east. It is forbidden to go to any of the Dead Places except to search for metal, and then he who touches the metal must be a priest or the son of a priest. Afterward, both the man and the metal must be purified.

These are the rules and the laws; they are well made. It is strictly forbidden to cross the great river and look upon the Place of the Gods. We do not even say its name, though we know its name. It is there that spirits live, and demons—and there are the ashes of the Great Burning.

My father is a priest; I am the son of a priest. I have been in the Dead Places near us with my father. At first, I was afraid. When he went into a dead house—a spirit house—to search for metal, I stood by the door, and my heart felt small and weak. The house did not have the smell of man, and there were old bones in a corner. But it is not fitting for a priest's son to show fear. I looked at the bones in the shadow and kept my voice still.

Then my father came out with the metal—a good, strong piece. I had not run away. He gave me the metal to hold. I took it and did not die. So he knew that I was truly his son and would be a priest in my time. That was when I was very young. After that, they gave me the good piece of meat and the warm corner by the fire.

In time, I myself was allowed to go into the dead houses and search for metal. So I learned the ways of those houses—and if I saw bones, I was no longer afraid. The bones are light and old, sometimes they fall into dust if you touch them. But touching them is a great sin.

I was taught the chants and the spells. I was taught how to stop the running of blood from a wound and many secrets. I liked to hear of the Old Days and the stories of the gods. I was taught how to read in the old books and how to make the old writings. My knowledge made me happy—like a fire in my heart.

But the old writings are hard to understand. I asked myself many questions that I could not answer. My lack of knowledge burned in me, and I wished to know more. At night, I would lie awake and listen to the wind. It seemed to me that it was the voice of the gods as they flew through the air.

When I was a man at last, I came to my father and said, "It is time for me to go on my journey. Give me your leave."

He looked at me for a long time, stroking his beard, then said at last, "Yes. It is time." That night, in the house of the priesthood, I received purification. My body hurt, but my spirit was a cool stone.

My father questioned me about my dreams. He bade me look into the smoke of the fire and see. I told what I saw—a river, and beyond it, a great Dead Place, and in it, the gods walking. I have always thought about that. The smoke waved and my head felt light. In the outer chamber, they were singing the Star song; it was like the buzzing of bees in my head.

Father asked me how the gods were dressed, and I told him. We know from the book, but I saw them as if they were before me. When I had finished, he threw the sticks three times and studied them as they fell.

"This is a very strong dream," he said. "It may eat you up."

"I am not afraid," I said.

He touched me on the breast and the forehead. He gave me the bow and three arrows.

"Take them," he said. "It is forbidden to travel east, forbidden to cross the river, forbidden to go to the Place of the Gods."

"All these things are forbidden," I said, but only my voice spoke, not my spirit.

"My son," he said, "if your dreams do not eat you up, you may be a great priest. If they eat you, you are still my son. Now go."

I set out, fasting as I went, as is the law. When the dawn came, I was out of sight of the village. I prayed and purified myself, waiting for a sign. The sign was an eagle. It flew east.

Sometimes, though, signs are sent by bad spirits. I waited again on the flat rock, fasting till the sun was beginning to sink. Then three deer passed in the valley. They too were going east. There was a white fawn with them, a very great sign.

I followed them. My heart was troubled about going east, yet I knew that I must go. My head hummed with my fasting so that, at first, I did not see the panther spring upon the white fawn. But before I knew it, the bow was in my hand, and the arrow went through the panther's eye and into his brain. He died as he tried to spring, and rolled over, tearing at the ground. Then I knew I was meant to go east. When night came, I made my fire and roasted meat.

It is eight-suns' journey to the east, and a man passes by many Dead Places. In one dead house, I found a good knife, and it made my heart feel big. Always when I looked for game, it was in front of my arrow. So I knew my magic was strong and my journey clean, in spite of the law.

Toward the setting of the eighth sun, I came to the banks of the great river. I had left the god-roads, for they had fallen apart into great blocks of stone. A long way off, I had seen the water through trees. At last, I came out upon an open place at the top of a cliff. There was the great river below, like a giant in the sun, very long, very wide. It could eat all the streams we know and still be thirsty. Its name Ou-dis-sun, the Sacred, the Long. No man of my tribe had seen it, not even my father, the priest. It was magic and I prayed. Then I raised my eyes and looked south. It was there—the Place of the Gods.

How can I tell what it was like? The red light was upon the towers, mighty and ruined. They were too big to be houses. I knew in a moment the gods would see me. I covered my eyes with my hands and crept back into the forest.

Surely, seeing that place was enough to do, and live. "My journey has been clean. Now I will go home," I thought. But I knew I could not. I knew I should have to cross the river and walk in the places of the gods, even if the gods ate me up.

There was a fire in my mind. If I went there, I would surely die, but if I did not go, I could never be at peace with my spirit again. It is better to lose one's life than one's spirit, especially if one is a priest and the son of a priest.

As I made the raft, the tears ran out of my eyes. I painted myself for death. My heart was cold as a frog and my knees like water, but the burning in my mind would not let me have peace. As I pushed the raft from the shore, I began my death song:

I am John, son of John and my people are the Hill people.
It is forbidden to go east, but I have gone,
Forbidden to go on the great river, but I am there.
Open your heart, you spirits, and hear my song.
My limbs are weak, but my heart is big
As I go to the Place of the Gods.

0   0   0

I was afraid. The current of the great river is very strong. It gripped my raft with its hands. I could feel evil spirits about me. I could feel their breath on my neck as I was swept downstream. Never have I been so much alone. I tried to think of my knowledge, but it was a squirrel's heap of winter nuts. I felt small and naked as a new-hatched bird, alone upon the great river.

After a while, my eyes were opened and I saw both banks of the river, with what had once been god-roads across it, though now they were broken and fallen like broken vines. They were broken in the time of the Great Burning, when fire fell out of the sky. Always the current took me nearer to the Place of the Gods, and huge ruins rose before my eyes.

I tried to guide my raft with the pole, but it spun around. I thought the river meant to take me past the Place of the Gods and out into the bitter Water of Legends. I grew angry and said aloud, "I am a priest and the son of a priest!" The gods heard me and showed me how to paddle. The current changed itself.

But as I drew near, my raft struck something and turned over. A great spike of rusted metal was sticking out, so I swam to it and hauled myself up and sat there panting. All I had managed to save was my bow, two arrows, and the knife. My raft went whirling downstream. I thought, *If it had trod me under, at least I would be safely dead.*

When my bow dried, I restrung it and walked on the Place of the Gods.

The ground underfoot did not burn me, as the tales say. It is not true either that it is an island covered with fogs and enchantment. It is not. It is a great Dead Place. Everywhere in it there are god-roads, cracked and broken. Everywhere there are ruins of the high towers of the gods. But they are not all broken. Here and there one still stands, like a great tree in a forest, and the birds nest high. But the towers look blind, for the gods are gone.

I saw a fish hawk, catching fish in the river. I saw a little dance of white butterflies over a heap of broken stones and columns. Just below them there was a carved stone broken in half, with cut letters. I can read, but I could not understand these. They said UBTREA. There was also the shattered image of a man or a god, made of white stone, and he wore his hair tied back like a woman's. His name was ASHING. I thought it wise to pray to ASHING.

I went north and did not try to hide myself. When a god or demon saw me, I would die, but meanwhile, my hunger for knowledge burned in me. Soon my belly was hungry too, but I did not hunt, for it is known the gods got their food from enchanted boxes and jars. When I was a child, I found one once and tasted it and found it sweet, but my father punished me, for others that food is death. Now, though, I had long gone past what was forbidden, and I entered the likeliest tower looking for the food of the gods.

I found it at last in the ruins of a great temple in the mid-city. The roof was painted like the night sky with its stars. My path led down into great caves and tunnels. But when I started to climb down, I heard the squeaking of rats, many tribes of unclean rats.

Finally, I found the food behind a door that still opened. I ate only fruits from the jars—a very sweet taste. There was drink too, in bottles of glass. The drink of the gods was strong and made my head swim. Soon I fell asleep on top of a stone.

When I awoke, the sun was low. Looking down, I saw a dog sitting on his haunches, his tongue hanging out of his mouth. He was as big as a wolf, with a gray-brown coat. I sprang up and shouted at him, but he was not afraid of me. He looked at me as if I were meat.

I reached for a stone and threw it, and he moved swiftly, but not far. Keeping to the heights of the ruins, I went toward a great broken god-road leading north. The dog followed, and there were others behind him. If I had slept later, they would have come upon me asleep and torn out my throat.

As I approached a dead house, the dogs suddenly decided to charge. I ran as fast as I could, looking for a door that would open. The dogs were snarling as they ran, and gaining speed! I did not stop. They were right behind me.

Finally I found a good door of strong metal. Ha! The dogs were surprised when I shut the door in their faces!

Now I was in darkness. I found stairs and climbed, turning around till my head was dizzy. At the top was another door. I opened it and found myself in a small chamber, with a bronze door on one side that had no handle. Perhaps there was a magic word to open it, but I did not have the word.

On the opposite wall was a door that led to a place of great riches. The god who lived there must have been a powerful god. I told the spirits of the place that I came in peace and not as a robber.

It was close and dry and dusty in the house of the gods. The magic was not gone from that place. I felt the spirits about me, weighing upon me.

Tonight I must sleep in a Dead Place! I thought. In spite of my wish for knowledge, the idea made

my tongue feel dry in my throat. Almost I would
have gone down and faced the dogs, but I did not.
I found a place to make a fire, wrapped myself in a
floor-covering, and slept in front of the fire.

Now I tell what is very strong magic: I woke in
the midst of the night. The fire had gone out, and I
was cold. It seemed that all around me were whis-
perings and voices. I closed my eyes to block them
out. Some will say that I slept again, but I do not
think I did. Why should I lie about it? If there are
spirits in the small Dead Places near home, what
spirits must there be in the great Place of the Gods?

I could feel the spirits drawing my spirit out of
my body as a fish is drawn on a line. I stepped out
of my body—I could see it asleep on the floor, but
it was not I.

I was drawn to look from a window upon the
city of the gods. It should have been dark, but everywhere there were lights—lines of light, circles
and blurs of light. Ten thousand torches would not
have been the same. The sky was alight; you could
barely see the stars for the glow. I was seeing the
city as it had been when the gods were alive. It was
such a sight, I could not have seen it in the body,
my body would have died.

Everywhere went gods, on foot and in chariots, gods beyond number, and their chariots blocked

the streets. They had turned night to day for their pleasure. They did not sleep with the sun. The noise of their coming and going was the noise of many waters. It was magic what they could do.

I looked out another window. The great vines of their bridges and the god-roads were mended. Restless, restless were the gods and always in motion! They burrowed tunnels under rivers, they flew in the air. With unbelievable tools they did giant works. No part of the Earth was safe from them.

And always, as they labored, they feasted and made pleasure. There was a drum in their ears, the pulse of the giant city, beating, beating like a man's heart.

Were they happy? What is happiness to the gods? They were great, they were mighty, they were wonderful and terrible. I saw them with wisdom beyond wisdom and knowledge beyond knowledge. And yet not all they did was well done.

Then I saw their fate come upon them, and that was terrible past speech. When gods war with gods, they use weapons we do not know. It was the falling out of the sky and a mist that poisoned. It was the time of the Great Burning and the Destruction. They ran about like ants in the streets—poor gods! And even after the city had become a Dead Place, for many years the poison was still in the ground. I saw the last of them die. Darkness came over the city, and I wept.

◦ ◦ ◦

When I awoke in the morning, my heart was perplexed. I knew the reason for the Dead Places, but it seemed it should not have happened, with all the magic they had. I went through the house looking for an answer.

Then I saw the dead god.

He was sitting in his chair by a window, looking out over the city. I thought he was alive; then I saw the skin on the back of his hand—it was like dry leather. The room was shut, hot and dry, and no doubt that had kept him as he was.

He was dressed in the clothes of the gods. I could not tell his age, but there was wisdom in this face, and great sadness. He had sat at his window watching his city die, and then he himself had died. But it is better to lose one life's than one's spirit—and you could see from the face that his spirit had not been lost. I knew that if I touched him he would fall into dust—and yet there was something unconquered in his face.

Then I knew that he was a man. I knew they had been neither gods nor demons, but men. It is a great knowledge. They were men. They went down a dark road, but they were men. I had no fear after that.

I went home. And when I saw my father again I said, "Father, I have been in the Place of the Gods and seen it! Slay me, if it is the law, but still I know— they were men!"

He looked at me out of both eyes. "The law is not always the same shape," he said. "I could not have done it in my time, but you have. Tell me."

I told, and I wished to tell all the people, but he said, "The truth is a hard deer to hunt. If you eat too much truth at once, you may die of the truth. It is better the truth should come little by little. Perhaps, in the old days, they ate knowledge too fast."

Nevertheless, we make a beginning. Now it is not for the metal alone that we go to the dead places—there are the books and the writings. We looks at the magic tools and we wonder.

When I am chief priest, we shall go beyond the great river, to the Place of the Gods, to the place newyork. We shall look for the images of the gods and find ASHING and the others, the gods Lincoln and Baltimore and Moses. But they were men who built the city, not gods or demons. I remember the dead man's face. They were men who were here before us. We must build again.